"How about that' ~~some kind of reco~~

"A record?" he asked.

Alex nodded. "We've been talking for fifteen minutes and haven't argued yet."

Wyatt laughed, realizing she was right. "I'd better leave then, before the moment is ruined." Amusement played along his lips.

"Good idea."

"More agreement. This *is* some kind of record," he marveled. He hesitated, overcome by bittersweet emotion before adding, "Too bad my dad's not around to see it."

Alex ached for his loss—and for her own. "Yes, too bad," she echoed sadly.

Looking back, Wyatt wasn't sure just what came over him. A wave of gratitude, no doubt. That and the devastating assaults of sorrow he was experiencing mingled together, temporarily taking away his ability to cope, to maintain a tight rein over himself.

It was as good an excuse as any.

Leaning forward, he placed his hand on her shoulder and then lightly brushed his lips against hers....

Dear Reader,

Welcome to a brand-new line and a brand-new family. I'm proud to be part of the launch of Harlequin Heartwarming originals.

This exciting new series inspired me to create the world of these four sisters helping their father run the inn that has been in their family for over 100 years.

I've often wondered what it might be like to run a bed-and-breakfast inn, something far more intimate than a hotel and a great deal more structured than, say, a frat house or hosting a group of relatives for the holidays. What sort of people would willingly do that? What kind of history would the inn that they're running have? Would it be brand-new, entrenched in the history of the area, or–? I decided to arm myself with several books describing the various bed-and-breakfast inns of this country, then progressed to the internet for more recent photos of several of these places. What you have before you is the result, detailing life in one such inn for one such family. I hope you enjoy the result and that you all get a chance to someday take a little time and spend a weekend or so in a bed-and-breakfast inn–at the very least, having someone serve you a homemade breakfast and make your bed for you would be a pleasant change from your everyday life.

As always, I thank you for taking the time to read my book, and from the bottom of my heart I wish you someone to love who loves you back.

All the best,

Marie Ferrarella

HARLEQUIN HEARTWARMING

USA TODAY Bestselling Author

Marie Ferrarella

Innkeeper's Daughter

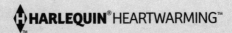

Recycling programs
for this product may
not exist in your area.

ISBN-13: 978-0-373-36629-3

INNKEEPER'S DAUGHTER

Copyright © 2013 by Marie Rydzynski-Ferrarella

Printed in U.S.A.

® HARLEQUIN®
www.Harlequin.com

MARIE FERRARELLA

earned a master's degree in Shakespearean comedy and, perhaps as a result, her writing is distinguished by humor and natural dialogue. This RITA® Award-winning author's goal is to entertain and to make people laugh and feel good. She has written over 240 books for Harlequin/Silhouette, some under the name Marie Nicole. Her romances are beloved by fans worldwide and have been translated into Spanish, Italian, German, Russian, Polish, Japanese and Korean. As of January 2013, she has been published by Harlequin for thirty years.

To
Marsha Zinberg,
with
deep affection
and respect

PROLOGUE

THE PATH FROM the back of the Ladera-by-the-Sea Inn to the small, private family cemetery seemed longer somehow today. Even though, as the inn's current owner and head of the Roman family, he'd walked it countless times, especially in the twelve years since his Amy had been laid to rest. He came here whenever he wanted to share a moment or to just feel close to his late wife. To remember a time when he and Amy used to walk hand in hand here, content just to listen to the sound of the waves caressing the shore.

Today it was to share the news he'd just received by phone, and his heartache.

Richard stood in front of his wife's tombstone the way he had so many countless times before, searching for a way to begin, to pour out what was in his heart without breaking down. He needed to hold himself together, to remain strong because he wasn't the only one who mattered, here.

His daughters didn't know yet, didn't know that the man they had always known and loved as Uncle Dan was gone.

"I guess you know, don't you?" Richard said to his wife, staring at her name on the tombstone, his voice throbbing with emotion though it was hardly above a whisper. "You're going to have company soon. He's finally gone."

For a moment he was almost overwhelmed by the dark sadness he felt and had to pause before continuing.

"My best friend died last night at 10:05. I know it's better this way, better for him, because he won't be hurting anymore. I know it got pretty bad toward the end, even though he wouldn't admit it. I should be happy for him, but he left this world far too soon and I feel so incredibly alone.

"Oh, I know, I know," Richard continued, anticipating exactly what his wife would have said if she were the one right in front of him instead of her tombstone. "I've got the girls and I love them all dearly, but it's just…not the same thing. They're all fine, independent young women now and I don't know what I'd do without them, but…I don't share the same history with them as I did with Dan." He pressed his lips together, taking a deep breath. "As I did with you."

He sighed. Granted, sometimes he hadn't seen Dan for months at a time because Dan's work had taken him all over the world, but he'd always been able to reach his best friend by phone. Or at least almost always.

Dan was also the very last fragment he had left of Amy. He and Dan had known each other since childhood, which meant Dan had also become Amy's friend long before Richard had married her.

In losing Dan, he'd lost another piece of Amy.

"Dan had this crazy idea…." A sad smile creased his lips. "You know how he always hoped that his Wyatt and our Alex would get married someday? And I told him it was never going to happen because those two would never stop locking horns long enough to fall in love? Well, he came up with a plan shortly after he was diagnosed with that awful disease. He didn't live long enough to watch it bear fruit, but he made sure he launched it. Even in his weakened state, he managed to drive himself from Southern California north more than two hours to Hollywood last week— only a week before he died.... I don't know how he did it."

Richard shut his eyes, shook his head.

"Poor Wyatt thought his dad was coming to spend a few days with him—that he'd get to show him an insider's view of Hollywood—before they both drove here for their annual vacation at the inn. Wyatt told me over the phone he was stunned when he saw Dan's deteriorated condition. More stunned, he said, when his dad told him he was going to the hospital, that he was dying…and that he wanted to ask him for one last favor."

Richard knew the disease had moved fast, but still, he couldn't imagine how difficult it would be for a father to keep it from his only son until the week before he died.

A sad smile continued to play on his lips. "Dan left it up to me to stand on the sidelines like some sort of invisible puppeteer and see it through." He laughed then, a small, aching laugh as he shook his head. "Dan could always get me to do anything he wanted. He had that way with people."

Richard glanced over his shoulder at the inn that had been in his family for generations. "I'd better be getting back. Wyatt's coming to tell me the news of his dad's passing. He isn't aware that I already know."

He and Wyatt had spoken after Wyatt had helped Dan check into the hospital a few days ago. But it was Dan's attending physician who had phoned Richard last night. At 10:05 precisely. Leaving nothing to chance, Dan had given the doctor instructions to alert Richard the moment he took his last breath.

"I'll keep you posted, Amy," Richard promised. Before turning to walk up to the inn, he added, "I love you.... And if you have any influence up there, get someone to help Alex open herself to the notion of doing something other than working. After Dan's deathbed wish, we're going to need all the help we can get down here. If his plan's going to work."

Taking another deep breath as he looked up toward the inn, Richard started back.

CHAPTER ONE

THE OLD VICTORIAN-STYLE bed-and-breakfast inn played a part in Alexandra Roman's earliest memories.

Majestic and regal, the Wedgwood blue-and-white building had seen its share of history. A more compact version had been standing there long before she was born and, Alex had no doubt, the inn would continue to be there long after she was gone.

Unless, of course, it was torn down for having been transformed into a nauseating eyesore because her father, in one of his never-ending bouts of kindheartedness, had given the go-ahead to a fast-talking general contractor whose taste, she was more than certain, began and ended in his mouth.

Periodically, Ladera-by-the-Sea, the 119-year-old bed-and-breakfast Alex's father owned and ran, underwent renovations. Those renovations either involved expansion—which took place when business was booming—or inevitable repairs as they became necessary.

Sometimes both.

This time, they seemed to also involve a contractor who admittedly spoke only one language—English—but for some reason, did not seem to understand the word "no." No matter how many times she repeated it.

Or how loudly.

When J. D. Clarke smiled, it always looked like a sneer to her—and he was smiling now. However, at this point, the smile—in *any* form—was wearing a little thin.

As thin as Alex's patience.

Taking off the baseball cap that pledged his allegiance to the San Diego Padres, Clarke wiped his damp brow, then repositioned the cap on his completely hairless head.

"Look, trust me, honey, you're gonna love the changes. All we need to do is knock out that wall..." He pointed vaguely in the direction of the load-bearing wall that separated the reception area from the dining room. "And then you'll have—"

"What I'll have is a huge gaping hole I not only will not 'love' but also definitely don't want." Alex narrowed her sharp blue eyes as she did her best *not* to glare at a man she found to be incredibly annoying. "Do you even *realize* that's a load-bearing wall?" she questioned. Not leaving him time to answer, Alex continued her verbal assault to get him to back off. "You're not knocking out anything. I am not your 'honey.' And I have no reason to trust you since you won't listen to reason and seem to have only *half* the attention span of a mentally challenged striped shoelace."

Clarke stared at her as he obviously attempted to untangle her last sentence so he could strike it down. But he failed. What he *didn't* fail at was displaying his contempt for her and her opinion. His smile was now very much a sneer.

"Look, lady, your father told me to use my judgment—"

Alex cut him short before Clarke could

get going. "That was when my father believed you had some, which, looking at those scribbles you showed me that you call 'plans'—" she waved at the papers he had spread out on the reception desk "—you clearly do not."

The smile/sneer completely vanished, replaced by an angry scowl. "I intended to show these to your father before you cornered me," he accused her. "And if you think I'm just going to stand here and be insulted—"

"No," she informed him sweetly. "What I think is that you and your oversize ego should be getting ready to leave now. I'm really hoping I'm right about that."

There was neither patience nor friendliness in her voice. Those had become casualties in the last volley of words. It never ceased to amaze her how her father could see the good in everyone, including someone who was so obviously a con artist. Her father definitely belonged in a gentler, kinder era. Possibly the era that had seen the original construction of the building they were presently living in and running as an inn.

Her father also seemed to be preoccupied lately. Something was bothering him, which would account for why he'd agreed to contract this renovator without a more detailed quote and then approve his renovation plans after the fact. That meant it was up to her to make sure the contractor was reined in—or, in this case, sent packing.

She saw it as her job to protect her father. The way she had from the moment her mother had died.

His chunky legs spread wide apart, Clarke took a stance that fairly shouted, "I'm not going anywhere." His words reinforced his body language.

"I take my orders from your father," the contractor said haughtily, as if that was going to make her instantly retreat.

The smile that curved Alex's mouth had no humor behind it. "That might be true. However, I'm the one who writes all the checks, Mr. Clarke. You want to get paid, you either agree to work with me—and I do *not* approve of this particular set of reno-

vation plans—or you take your 'helpers'—
you can't miss them, they're the ones who
have been doing an incredible imitation of
'still life' around the inn for the past week
and a half—and your scribbled cartoons,
and *leave. Now.*" Her smile, no more genuine than Clarke's, returned. "The choice
is yours."

J. D. Clarke scowled at the tall, willowy blonde with the viper tongue, clearly
weighing his options.

She could almost read his thoughts. She
was the owner's daughter, but she didn't
exactly pose a physical threat to him. For a
moment, Alex suspected he might actually
try to physically confront her. She almost
welcomed the idea. Then she'd show him
precisely what kind of physical threat she
could prove to be. *Bring it on, guy!*

Before he could take a step, however,
Dorothy came into the reception area. Alex
saw the older woman at the same time the
contractor did. Their head housekeeper was
staring straight at the man and Dorothy
didn't look any friendlier than she must've.
Dorothy, with her gray hair pulled back,

could appear rather formidable when she wanted to. And she had the unquestioning loyalty of a German shepherd to the Roman family, even though, when it came to animals, she resembled a Saint Bernard a lot more than she did a German shepherd. A rather large Saint Bernard.

Her very body language announced just whose side, sight unseen, she was taking.

"Is there a problem, Miss Alex?" she asked, her deep gray eyes fixed on Clarke. She made no attempt to hide her contempt. Time and again, thought Alex, she had demonstrated she had no use for people who didn't show the proper respect for her family.

She shook her head. "No, no problem, Dorothy. Right, Mr. Clarke?" she asked pointedly, sparing the man a quick glance.

"Right." The contractor bit off and spat out the word as if it had been dipped in sardine oil that had gone bad months ago.

Muttering under his breath about having to deal with crazy women, Clarke collected his papers that illustrated the new—and pricey—"vision" he had for the inn, tucked them under his arm and marched toward the front door.

"I'm still sending you a bill," he declared, tossing the words over his shoulder as he paused for a beat at the threshold to the inn.

"And I'll be sure to look it over closely," Alex informed him amiably.

"Your father should have had sons," Clarke said as if he was uttering a curse. With that, he stomped out of the building.

He certainly wanted them, Alex couldn't help thinking. Her expression remained unchanged, giving no hint to her thoughts or that the disgruntled contractor had managed, through sheer dumb luck, to hit her exactly where she lived. It was a sore spot for her.

Dorothy took a step forward, her shoulders tensed, braced. Everything about her declared that she intended to make the man literally eat his words or cough up a serious apology. But Alex put a hand out to stop the woman before Dorothy could go after the contractor.

Instead she shook her head at Dorothy

and raised her voice to call after the departing man, "I'll pass that along to him, Mr. Clarke. I'm sure my father will give your comment all the attention it deserves."

Now out of sight, they could hear Clarke gathering his team as he stormed off.

Dorothy turned and studied her. The woman had watched her grow from a gangly, awkward preteen into the poised, self-confident young adult she hoped people saw her as now.... She sure worked hard enough to convey that image.

"Why did you stop me?" she asked. Alex knew that she and her three younger sisters were like daughters to Dorothy, who had no family to call her own. And since their mother's death, they were even more glad to have Dorothy in their lives. "I just wanted five minutes alone with him."

Alex laughed, shaking her head. She knew the offer came from the woman's very large heart, but it was still better not to allow that sort of one-on-one "meeting" to take place.

"That's four and a half minutes more

than he could have handled, Dorothy," Alex told her with a wink.

Though polite, Dorothy was clearly angry. "He had no right to talk to you like that. He deserved to be put in his place," she said with feeling.

Alex flashed a smile at the older woman. This time there was absolutely nothing forced about it. Dorothy was one of the good ones. Like her father. "I appreciate you standing by me."

Dorothy laughed softly, shrugging off the thanks. "Not that you needed it. You fight your own battles well enough. You always have." Seemingly without realizing it, as she spoke she fisted her hands at her sides. "It's just that seeing him trying to put you down made me so angry—that fool isn't good enough to lick your boots." Dorothy glanced down at her feet. "Or high heels, as the case might be. So he's gone for good, right?" she asked, just to be certain that there was no need for her to hang around.

"Right," Alex confirmed. "Seems Clarke had a totally different vision for where the inn should be going than what was established by the family years ago."

Ladera-by-the-Sea Inn had begun as a modest little five-bedroom home, converted into an inn as an attempt by Ruth Roman, the original owner, to keep a roof over her children's heads after her husband was brought down by a stray bullet fired during a heated dispute between two other men.

Over the years, as different generations came to helm the inn, more rooms were added. Slowly, more rooms turned into wings, then modest guest houses until the inn seemed to become its own miniature village, but always with a single, distinguished Victorian motif. A motif that Clarke was obviously determined to change, turning the inn into a hodgepodge of old and modern, that would have resembled nothing specific and been part fish, part fowl and all very off-putting.

Clarke had seen it as making a statement. And who knows? Maybe he might even have convinced her father, who didn't have a strong sense of design. That would have been criminal. Of course, Alex would have been able to convince her dad of that. In her emotional reaction to seeing Clarke's plans first, she'd just skipped that step.

As far as Alex was concerned, her statement said, "Your services are no longer needed," in a loud, clear voice.

"That kind always think they know best," Dorothy sniffed, shaking her head as she looked off in the direction that Clarke had taken. "You can do much better than the likes of him." She sighed. "Your father's just too kindhearted, giving anyone work who shows up on his doorstep with a sad story."

The woman pressed her lips together. She had to know how that sounded. But Alex knew Dorothy hadn't meant to be critical of her dad, the man she looked up to and respected more than anyone else. "Of course, I shouldn't talk. If it wasn't for that wonderful man, heaven only knows where I'd be right now."

Alex didn't want Dorothy to dwell on the past, or what had initially brought her, destitute and desperate, to the inn.

"Well, all I know is we'd be lost without you, so there's no use in speculating about a state of affairs that mercifully never came about." She squeezed the woman's hand. "We all love you, Dorothy. You mean the world to us."

The other woman blushed.

Dorothea O'Hara had been a guest at the inn some twelve years ago. Down on her luck, abandoned by the man she'd given her heart—and her savings—to, she had checked into the inn, wanting to spend one final night somewhere warm and inviting. Before she ended her emotional suffering by taking sleeping pills. After the fact, Dorothy had been quite frank about her intentions, much to the upset of the Romans.

Years later Richard told his daughters he must have subconsciously sensed how unhappy Dorothy had been because something had prompted him to knock on her door that evening and engage her in a conversation that went on for hours.

Newly widowed, he'd talked about his four daughters, about the adjustments all five of them had had to make because of his wife's sudden passing, about how strange life had seemed to him at first without the woman he loved by his side.

He'd talked about everything and anything until the first rays of the morning sun came into Dorothy's room.

For Dorothy, dawn had brought with it a realization that she was still alive—and still without options. She confessed to the man she'd been talking to all night that she wasn't going to be able to pay for her stay.

Embarrassed, she'd offered to work off her tab.

It hadn't taken long for her to work off the debt. Once she had, Richard told her that if she didn't have anywhere else to go, he would consider it a personal favor if she stayed on at the inn.

She'd quickly become family. As had some of the other guests at the inn who were initially only passing through.

The inn, Alex firmly believed, was the richer for it.

But there were times, few and far between, when her father made a mistake, a bad judgment call. This latest contractor had been one of those calls.

Christina Roman MacDonald walked in, munching on an apple. Alex knew her sister would have preferred a breakfast pastry— one of her specialties as the inn's resident chef and one of the most requested items on the breakfast menu. But she was trying to instill healthy eating habits in Ricky, her four-year-old son, and that meant apples rather than pastries.

Swallowing what she'd been chewing, she said, "Hey, I just saw J.D. and his motley crew climbing into that beat-up truck of his. The guy almost ran right over me to get to it." It wasn't a complaint, just an observation. "Fastest I've seen the lot of them moving since they got here last week." Cris nodded in the direction of the rear of the inn. "What's up?"

"Miss Alex's temper," Dorothy told her. There was no small note of pride in the woman's voice. "She finally got fed up with that so-called contractor's grand plans."

Leaning forward, the heavyset woman confided in as close to a whisper as she could manage, which meant it could undoubtedly be heard in the center of the closest San Diego shopping center, "No disrespect intended, Miss Alex, but it certainly took you long enough. The man was charging you for breathing—times five, since he was also padding the bill to pay for those five 'helpers' of his."

"Now," Cris pointed out, "they *did* work sometimes."

"Yeah," Dorothy snorted, "every time your father walked by."

"Well, the main thing is that they're gone and we won't have to put up with them any longer," Alex said, trying to put an end to the matter. Of course, they still had to deal with the contract her father had signed, but in it her father had outlined specific things he'd wanted done. Clarke's plans strayed dramatically from the contract. The fact that he'd backed down so easily—without first speaking to her father—clearly told her that she was right.

"Yeah." Cris nodded, regarding what was left of her apple as if she was seeking the answers to the mysteries of the universe. "Now all you have to do is explain all this to Dad."

Dorothy waved her hand at the problem, dismissing it. "Mr. Roman's a saint," she proclaimed with feeling. "He'll understand that you were just looking out for him, Miss Alex."

"Or overriding him," Cris chimed in with a barely suppressed grin.

"It's not like that," Alex protested. "I wasn't overriding him. If Dad was just a little bit tougher, I wouldn't have to be so vigilant." It wasn't that her father was a pushover or easily hoodwinked, it was just that he saw the best in everyone, even in those who didn't seem to have a decent bone in their bodies. "There are times when I think that he could just *give* the inn away if it wasn't for us."

"For you," Cris corrected her pointedly. They all knew that Alex was the fighter, the one who led the cavalry charge if a charge needed to be led. "The rest of us would just let Dad be Dad. I guess what I'm saying is, thanks for handling all that so we don't have to." And then she nodded. "He really is just too darn nice for his own good."

"Who is?" Richard inquired, walking into the reception area and crossing over to join his two eldest daughters. He nodded at the housekeeper. "Morning, Dorothy."

She could have tried to bury it in rhetoric, but what was the point? Alex thought. She believed in being honest.

"You," Alex told her father without any hesitation.

He knew that look. For a moment he allowed himself to be sidetracked. What he'd come in to tell his daughters could wait a few minutes. It didn't change anything, but keeping the news from them even a moment longer was a moment they were spared from dealing with what he had to tell them.

"Why do I get the feeling that my eldest daughter is about to sit me down for a lecture?" he asked with a smile.

Alex shook her head. "No, no lecture, Dad."

"But she does have some news to pass

on," Cris informed their father when Alex said nothing to follow up her simple denial.

"Oh?" Richard turned to his eldest child. There were times she was so much like her mother, it gave him both pleasure and pain to look at her. Pleasure to remember all the good times they had shared together and pain because the time he had to remember was so very short in comparison to the rest of his life.

He spared Dorothy a glance as he waited for Alex to enlighten him. The housekeeper's face was an open book and if there was something he really needed to know, he would be able to see it in her expression.

When the woman who never failed to let him know that he had saved her life that night they'd talked until dawn averted her face so he couldn't look into it, Richard knew the news couldn't be good.

Did they already know?

No, Richard decided. What he saw in his daughters' faces was discomfort, not sorrow or despair.

Looking at Alex, he said, "I'm listening."

CHAPTER TWO

ALEX COULD FEEL three pairs of eyes on her, waiting expectantly. Dorothy and Cris obviously already knew what she had to say and were there to hear her father's reaction. Her father didn't know what was coming, although, she now noticed, he seemed really sad.

Maybe she shouldn't have jumped the gun this way, firing Clarke like she had. In all her twenty-eight years, Alex couldn't remember a single instance when her father made her doubt herself, or gave her reason to believe he was disappointed in her. She had a degree in accounting, as well as one in hotel management. There was no reason in the world for her to even hesitate answering his question for a moment.

And yet, she did.

Her eyes never leaving his, she took a

deep breath, released it slowly and said, "I fired J. D. Clarke, Dad."

Richard seemed only mildly surprised by the news.

He was a little taken aback. He'd been consumed by his grief, but even if he hadn't been, he wouldn't have expected his daughter to override his decisions. Ordinarily, Alex would have consulted him before taking any sort of final action like this.

At least, he would have assumed that she would consult with him since, now that he thought about it, Alex had never fired anyone before. Oh, there had been times when she had complained at length about one person or another currently working at the inn, but those matters were always ultimately dealt with and straightened out. Most of the time, a simple one-on-one conversation resolved the problem. No one had ever been fired. The high employee turnaround was a result of their needs being seasonal. Most of the extra people who worked at the inn were there because they were down on their luck and he had taken them on until they were back on their feet again.

While all his daughters worked at the inn in some capacity, Alex was his second in charge and she took running the inn very seriously.

In fact, sometimes, he felt that she took her job too seriously. That was a real source of guilt for him because those were the times when he felt that he had stolen a very important part of his daughter's life from her.

The part where she got to enjoy herself without all these responsibilities hemming her in and making demands on her. It was his fault that things had arranged themselves this way. His health hadn't always been the best. After Amy had died, it was all he could do to pull himself together and do what needed to be done to take care of the girls.

Alex had been all of sixteen when—his health poor at the time—she appointed herself acting head of the family.

The problem was, she never really *un*-appointed herself acting head of the family and had just continued in that position from then on. She had even given up plans to attend an out-of-state college, electing, instead, to attend U.C. San Diego, living at home and juggling her studies with her duties on the home front.

There were times during this hectic interlude in her life that Richard had doubted his eldest daughter even slept. But she'd managed to do it all, help run the inn *and* graduate with honors despite all the demands on her time, which, among other things, included a double major.

These days, Alex's life was no less hectic. She continued to concern herself with the hundred and one minute, day-to-day details that went with running the inn. There was very little time for Alex to concern herself with just being Alex.

And that's why he had to hope that his friend Dan's little plan might stand a chance.

Richard studied her now, wondering what had set her off enough to make her actually fire someone. Whatever it was, he knew without being told that it was justified. But while he had tremendous faith in his daughter, he still needed to know the circumstances. And why she hadn't included him in the decision.

So, for a moment longer, he put off being the bearer of sad news and asked Alex, "Is there a particular reason why you fired him?"

Alex nodded her head, possibly a bit too emphatically.

"A very particular reason," she told him. There wasn't a sliver of uncertainty in her tone. He knew there were times she'd find herself second-guessing a situation, but not in this case. In this case, she was absolutely certain she'd done the right thing.

"Clarke was going to butcher the inn," Alex replied.

The general contractor had come to him with several letters of referral as well as half-a-dozen photographs of his work. All in all, the man had come across as a competent general contractor. Not to mention that Clarke had talked about being a family man, something Richard found to be rather important.

A family man who needed to provide for that family. For Richard, it had been a very important deciding factor in hiring the man.

He remembered as a boy listening to his own father tell him stories about his great-great-grandmother, Ruth, and how she'd converted her home into an inn to keep from losing it, as well as a way to provide for her five children.

Keeping those stories foremost in his mind was what had kept Richard from *ever* turning away a single person who needed a place to stay.

"And just how did J.D. intend to 'butcher' the inn?" he asked Alex.

"He didn't *intend* to do it," Alex corrected her father. "But that would have been the end result of what he was going to do to the inn."

Richard glanced at his other daughter and then at Dorothy, but there was no enlightenment from either quarter. "I don't think I understand."

To Alex, the inn was like a living, breathing entity. Something to watch over and protect so that it would be here, just as her ancestor had intended, for many, many years to come. J. D. Clarke, she was certain, had ideas that would've dramatically changed the direction the inn had been going for more than a hundred years. And his staff sure hadn't given her any confidence that they could do good work that would stand the test of time.

"You'd hired him to make additions to the inn. He took it upon himself to go in a whole different direction. He showed me these really awful sketches he planned on 'bringing to life,' as he put it. When I said they would clash with what was already here, he told me I'd change my mind once they were completed. I think he felt I was challenging his judgment and he wouldn't budge. So I fired him. He left me no choice."

Alex took the folded piece of paper she'd slipped under the sign-in ledger she kept on the desk and placed it in front of her father as exhibit A. It was the only one of Clarke's sketches he had left behind.

"It looked more like a growth than an

addition," she said indignantly, stabbing a finger at the drawing. "And it's *modern*." Alex all but spat the word out, as if it was a new strain of a fatal disease.

She watched her father glance over the sketch. By his expression, she could tell that he couldn't quite understand the problem.

"Dad, you *can't* just slap something that looks like it vacationed in the Museum of Modern Art onto a Victorian house. The two décors clash horribly and at the very least it would make us look…indecisive," she finally declared for lack of a better word, "to our guests."

"Indecisive?" Cris asked, puzzled. She pulled over the sketch to look at it herself.

Alex wanted support from her sister, not a challenge. "Shouldn't you be back in the kitchen, getting ready for the guests coming in for lunch?" she prompted.

"Got it covered," Cris told her cheerfully. "Go on, you were saying?" It was obvious that she wanted to see how far Alex was going to go with this.

Alex turned her attention back to her father, stating the rest of her case. "All the other additions over the years always retained that original Victorian flavor. It's what the guests who come here expect. Not to mention he was intending to knock down that wall. That wall," she emphasized, pointing to it. "That's load-bearing, isn't it? And if it isn't and I'm wrong about that, well, he sure didn't argue. Because he didn't know better. The guy didn't have a clue what he was doing. Besides," she added in a quieter but no less firm voice, "Clarke acted as if he thought he knew what was best for the inn."

"When we all know that *you* are the one who knows what's best for the inn," Cris declared solemnly, suppressing a grin.

Richard looked from one daughter to the other. He had devoted his life to raising his girls and was experienced enough to know that there was a confrontation in the making. His daughters loved one another, but that didn't keep them from going at it heatedly.

He headed the confrontation off before it could get under way.

Kissing Alex's forehead, he told her, "I trust you to make the right decisions. Of course, this means we're going to have to find another general contractor." He sighed, reminding her that the contractor had originally been called in to make some much needed repairs. Repairs that as of yet hadn't happened. "If we don't, then with the first big rain of the season we'll have an indoor pool in the kitchen, thanks to the fact that the roof has seen *much* better days."

"Why don't we use the one we had the last time?" Cris proposed. "Mr. Phelps was really nice," she added.

Alex looked at her. "Do you remember when the last time was?"

Thinking for a moment, Cris shrugged. Richard was only too aware that a great deal of life had happened to Cris since then so she couldn't really be expected to know the answer to that question. "Five, seven years ago?"

Alex shook her head. "Try ten."

"Okay, ten," Cris acknowledged. "So? What's the problem?"

Alex looked at her sister for a long moment. Didn't Cris think she would have gone back to the other man if that had actually been an option? "Other than the fact that he's dead, nothing."

"Dead?" Cris echoed in surprise. "When did that happen?"

"Around the same time he stopped breathing, I imagine. Give or take," Alex replied in the calm voice she used when she was trying to remove herself from a situation. Situations that usually only involved her sisters and came from being one of four kids. Growing up fighting to get an edge over the other three.

She expected her father to say something to rein her in, but he didn't. She found that a little odd.

"Very funny," Cris retorted, her expression indicating that was exactly what she *didn't* think it was.

Alex ignored her. "Don't worry, Dad, I'll find us another general contractor. One who listens to what the inn is trying to say."

Richard laughed shortly, but there was no humor in the sound. Alex picked up on it instantly.

"I'd settle for a contractor who doesn't charge an arm and a leg," her father said.

"No body limbs, just reasonable rates. Got it," Alex promised with a wink.

Cris glanced at the oversize watch on her wrist. It was large and bulky and made her seem even smaller and more fragile than she was. The only time she ever took it off was when she showered.

The watch chastened Alex and she regretted what she'd said to Cris. The watch had belonged to Mike. It was the last thing he'd given her before he'd left, saying that every time she looked at it, she should think of him and know that he was that much closer to coming home.

Except that he wasn't and he didn't.

Mike's unit had been called up and, just like that, he had been deployed to Iraq. He'd been there less than a week when a roadside bomb took him away from her permanently.

He'd died before he'd ever been able to hold his newborn son in his arms.

"Looks like I'm out of time," Cris murmured. She raised her deep blue eyes to look at Alex. "Looks like you get your wish, big sister. I'm out of here."

"No, wait." Richard held up his hand like an old-fashioned policeman charged with directing the flow of traffic.

"Sure," Cris answered after exchanging a look with Alex. Alex saw by her sister's expression that Cris had no more of a clue what was going on than she did. "Carlos can watch Ricky a few more minutes," she said, referring to the busboy who also helped out in the kitchen when things got a little too hectic at the inn. "What's up, Dad?"

"I came in to tell you girls that…" Richard hesitated and Alex could see that whatever was on his mind was not a subject he found easy to talk about.

"Well, I've got beds to make," Dorothy said to no one in particular, turning to leave the reception area. She clearly assumed that whatever their dad had to say was intended only for his family.

But she'd assumed wrong.

"Stay, please, Dorothy," Richard requested. "This concerns you, too."

"Of course, sir," Dorothy said politely, staying where she was.

An uneasy feeling feathered through Alex. "Okay, now you're scaring me, Dad," she told him.

This was the way she'd discovered her father was ill all those years ago. Fortunately his lung cancer was still in the early stages when it had been detected and she had done the research to find an excellent physician who was able to halt the progression of the disease and eventually get her father back on his feet.

"What's wrong?" Alex pressed, wanting him to get the information out *now.*

"Are you ill, Mr. Roman?" Dorothy asked, in concern and compassion.

"Dad?" Cris only uttered the single word, obviously too fearful to say any more. Probably, thought Alex, too afraid that if she said anything more out loud, it would come into being.

Apparently realizing how his request for their attention must have sounded to them, Richard was quick to set their minds at ease, at least about this one point.

"Oh, no, this doesn't have anything to do with me. At least, not in the way you might think. Although…"

As long as her father's cancer hadn't returned, she could handle anything else, Alex thought. Rolling her eyes dramatically, she said, "Dad, you are really, really bad at breaking news to people, you know that?" She shook her head. "C'mon, out with it."

He suddenly turned to Cris and asked, "Are Stephanie and Andrea around? If it's all the same with you, I'd really rather only have to say this once."

"Okay, back to being scared," Alex announced, trying to keep the situation light even though she was filled with a sense of foreboding and dread.

"I'll go find them," Dorothy volunteered.

But Alex was already on the inn's conference line, calling both her younger sisters' cell phones—something neither girl was ever without except, possibly, in the shower and not always then. She was convinced that Andy was hermetically sealed to hers.

"Stevi, Andy, Dad wants to see us at the reception desk. Now." It wasn't a request, it was an order, issued with an undercurrent of fear.

"Anyone ever tell you you make a great dictator?" Cris asked mildly.

Ordinarily that might have sparked an exchange that bordered on the lively, but right now, Alex paid no attention to her sister. She was focused on her father, to the exclusion of everything else.

"Do we get a hint, Dad? A glimmer of a coming attraction while we're waiting for the two divas to show up?" she prompted.

"It's not about me, I promise," Richard told her with what she assumed was his attempt at a reassuring smile. It didn't work.

"Or the inn?" Alex asked, watching her father's face. Family was exceedingly important to her, but the inn was a close second.

The next moment she told herself that it couldn't be about the inn. She handled all the accounts as well as the never-ending piles of paperwork that went along with running the place. She would have known if there was a lean on it or a second mortgage taken out—

Wouldn't she?

She looked uncertainly at her father.

"Or the inn," he assured her. Again, he qualified his answer a moment later. "At least, not in the way you mean it."

"All right, just how *does* it concern the inn?" Cris demanded, clearly not able to take another moment of suspense.

Without meaning to, Richard sighed. He'd left Wyatt sitting in his office. The young man had arrived quietly just a few minutes ago, entering through the gardens and the back door that was always unlocked during daylight hours. Guests hardly ever made use of that entrance, but friends did. And Wyatt was a friend. More like a son, actually. He'd known him since the day the boy had been born.

"Wyatt has come to see me. He's just arrived."

"Wyatt?" Alex echoed.

The name brought with it a legion of memories that ran the expanse of two decades and more. Theirs was an ongoing, antagonistic relationship that seemed to be the very embodiment of the war between the sexes—even though he got on well enough with her sisters and they with him. Complicating this was the fact that her heart never failed to skip a couple of beats the first time she saw him each year. Her physical reaction never changed. It was only when her mind kicked in that her behavior returned to normal. Wyatt Taylor was an extremely handsome example of the male gender and it was her misfortune to be attracted to a man she was constantly at odds with the rest of the time he was at the inn.

"When?" Alex wanted to know. "I didn't see him come in."

She'd never seen her father's smile look so incredibly sad. "He came in through the back."

"Why?" Alex asked. Whatever was bothering her father was tied to Wyatt, she thought. It figured.

Her sisters got along with Wyatt. For the most part, he was like their big brother.

The son her dad never got to have.... She refused to dwell on that.

Wyatt had been coming to the inn every summer with his father for years. She and the others all fondly thought of Wyatt's father as Uncle Dan, even though Dan Taylor was no relation to either of their parents. He and their father had been best friends since elementary school.

Daniel Taylor was an independent journalist who'd traveled the world over, hunting down stories that proved to be too challenging, too elusive for the new breed of reporter. His erratic lifestyle had put a very real strain on his marriage until one summer, Dan found himself divorced and much too far away from the son he adored. So every summer, when he was granted a month's precious custody, he would bring his son with him to the inn. He came here because his best friend was a single father, too, and was blessed with insight. He came because he wanted Wyatt to have fun with kids his own age, and she and her sisters qualified.

And above all else, he came to the inn

because he practically lived out of his suitcase and had no real place to call home. So for four weeks each summer, Ladera-by-the-Sea Inn became home to Dan and his son. And, by extension, she and her sisters, as well as her father, became Dan's missing family.

During the rest of the year, whenever he could, Dan would come to visit and stay a few days or a week—until another assignment would whisk him away. When they were younger, Dan brought gifts from the places he'd visited. As they grew older, Alex realized that the greatest gift the man had brought them was himself.

"Why isn't Wyatt out here?" Alex asked.

Whatever was wrong, she was convinced it had to do with Wyatt. Although for the life of her, she couldn't begin to guess what it could be.

"Because I told him to wait," Richard answered quietly.

"Why isn't Uncle Dan with him?" Cris asked suddenly.

And even as she asked the simple question, Alex knew the answer. She guessed by her sister's expression that Cris must have known it, too. If they were right, Alex hoped the news didn't take Cris back to the morning the chaplain and another soldier arrived on the inn's doorstep to tell her that although Mike was coming home from his mission, it wasn't the kind of homecoming they'd expected.

"This is about Uncle Dan, isn't it?" Cris asked quietly.

After a beat, her father nodded his head. His eyes followed his two youngest daughters as they walked into the reception area. "Yes," he said. "It is."

CHAPTER THREE

"UH-OH, THIS HAS the looks of something serious," Stephanie murmured to Andrea as they walked to the reception desk together. "You know what this is about?" she asked.

"When do I ever find out anything before you do?" Andy asked, lengthening her stride.

It was hard to miss the family resemblance, thought Alex, both the one to the other as well as to her and Cris, the older sisters. Approximately the same height, Stephanie and Andrea gave the impression of being tall and willowy, despite the fact that neither was more than five-six. Like her and Cris, both had straight, dark blond hair and captivating, magnetic blue eyes that seemed capable of looking into a person's soul. At least that's what everybody always told Alex.

"What did you do?" Andy asked Stevi.

"Me? Nothing. Why would you think it's me?"

"Well, it's not me," Andy said in an impatient whisper. "You called, Queen Bee?" she added to Alex in a louder, cheerful tone.

Stevi poked her younger sister in the ribs. Alex would agree with Stevi's silent message—this wasn't the time to be flippant.

"What's going on, Alex?" Andy asked. All traces of her flippant tone were gone.

"Dad, did something happen to Uncle Dan?" she asked. She wanted an answer, but she wanted to hear the *right* answer: that Daniel Taylor, the man who'd told her endless stories about places she knew she would never be able to visit, making them all seem so vivid and real to her, was all right. That the man who had just been here a few weeks ago wasn't here now, the way he always was at the first stroke of summer, because he'd finally met someone special and was taking some well-earned time off with her.

But the look on her father's face, the look of a man who was struggling to come to terms with losing part of himself, told her this had nothing to do with any newfound romance.

Afraid now, not for herself but for her father—and, although she'd never admit it out loud—for Wyatt, the boy she'd grown up with, she gently grasped her father's arm.

"Dad?"

His eldest daughter's tone said it all— "What is it?" "What happened?" and "How can I help?" all wrapped up in a single word.

"Pancreatic cancer," was all Richard trusted himself to say.

A minute more and maybe he would get better control over his emotions, but right now, those were the only words he was able to utter without breaking down. Dan had told him the moment he'd received the prognosis from his doctor. Come to him and asked him not to tell anyone else, not his daughters, not Wyatt. He didn't want to see pity marking his last few months, or however long he had. At the same time, he'd wanted an ally to help him maintain his facade—and he wanted his best friend to be prepared.

Dan's last visit had been a struggle. His friend had only had a few weeks left to live and he'd looked pale, his step less sure. But it really had seemed as if he was only a little tired. A force like Dan just didn't die.

The news of Dan's death, when it finally came from the attending physician last night, had still managed to hit him with the force of a sledgehammer.

Richard heard someone gasp and looked up to see that it was Stevi. He reached out to hold her tightly. Of the four of them, she was the most sensitive, the one whose threshold for emotional pain was far too low for her to function well in stressful situations.

For the most part, they were probably all overprotective of her—even Andy—sometimes keeping things from her rather than subjecting Stevi to undue emotional distress. Stevi had been the one who'd cried for days when their pet hamster had died.

When their mother had suddenly been taken from them, Stevi had stopped talking for a month. She'd been ten at the time.

He stepped back, gripped Stevi by the shoulders and studied her to make sure she'd be all right. Then he let her go as he took in the others, coming at last to Alex.

Alex's eyes had never left her father's stricken expression—how could she not have seen that? How could she have *missed* that pain, that sorrow? It was right there for her to see, she berated herself. What was she, blind?

"Is he—?"

Alex couldn't get herself to finish the sentence. She could feel her throat closing up, not just in sympathy for her father, but because she really, really loved Uncle Dan. They all did.

When she'd been very young, she'd had a crush on the man, daydreaming about going off with him to exotic parts unknown. It seemed hopelessly romantic to her to follow stories to wherever they might lead, no matter what the danger. As long as they had each other to lean on for support, things would work out.

It had irked her at the time that Wyatt looked so much like his father, especially since she and the younger Taylor got along like the proverbial cat and dog. Granted it had been mostly her doing, but that didn't change the outcome of antagonism. All those summers that Wyatt had spent at the inn, she'd found new and unique ways to torment him so that, somewhere along the line, Wyatt wouldn't usurp her in her father's eyes, becoming the son she felt certain he had always secretly longed for.

Once upon a time, she'd accidentally overheard her father talking to Uncle Dan about having a son. The exact words that had all but burned themselves into her brain had been, *You don't know how very lucky you are to have a son to share things with*. To her, there had been longing and a touch of envy in her father's voice. It said, in effect, that she could never measure up to his having a son. But it didn't keep her from trying, anyway.

Her less-than-easygoing past with Wyatt notwithstanding, she knew what it was like to lose a parent, knew the awful pain that caused, and she felt for Wyatt.

But predominantly she felt for her father.

Especially now, as she watched him grimly nod his head in response to the question she couldn't bring herself to complete.

"Yes," her father said hoarsely, "he's gone."

"But he was just here," Andy protested. "How could he die when he was just here?"

It was Dorothy who draped her arm comfortingly around the twenty-year-old's slim shoulders and murmured softly, "These things happen."

Alex shared a look with Cris, who bit her lower lip. Uncle Dan had been there for her sister when her husband had died halfway around the world. Although she and the rest of the family had done their best to be supportive of Cris, Dan had been able to supply something the others couldn't. He had actually been in the region where Mike had died and could by that very fact somehow

connect her to the place where Mike had
been permanently taken away from her.

It had meant a lot. They'd all recognized
that.

After a moment Cris was able to ask her
question. "When?"

"Very suddenly," her father answered
in a hushed, hoarse voice, unable to take
a deep breath because of the tremendous
weight he felt pressing down on his chest.
"Yesterday."

"Yesterday?" Stevi cried.

Dan was supposed to have arrived at the
inn yesterday with Wyatt. When he hadn't,
they had chalked it up to the fact that there
were times when Dan Taylor was not one
of the most punctual people.

"Where was he when…when it happened? Why didn't he come to us? Why
didn't he tell us? He must have known."

Stevi's questions tumbled out in rapid-
fire succession. Even so, they found no target, scattering to the corners of the room,
searching for any answers that made a
smattering of sense.

As her sisters closed ranks around their

father, alternating between asking questions and offering mutual comfort, Alex quietly took a step back.

And then another.

And another, until she'd managed to unobtrusively detach herself from the inner circle. Once certain that her sisters and Dorothy had surrounded their father with their love and overwhelming sympathy, Alex turned on her heel and quickly made her way to her father's small office at the back of the first floor.

About to knock lightly on the door before entering, she decided against it.

Instead she slowly pushed open the door, as if she was opening a portal to another world, a world currently filled to overflowing with grief.

Or so she imagined.

She found Wyatt standing at the window with his back to the door.

His body was rigid, as if he was attempting to shoulder something that was far too heavy for him to actually manage. A burden that threatened to bring him to his knees if he took as much as a step in any direction.

A minor tug-of-war took place inside Alex and then she decided to back out of the room, to wait until Wyatt was better equipped to deal with the offer of sympathy from others—especially her.

But as she placed her hand on the doorknob again, preparing to ease the door shut, she saw Wyatt raise his head just a fraction.

"Hello, Alex," he said in a quiet voice that sounded barely human.

Hearing him speak startled her. She stared at the back of his head. "How did you—?"

"Your reflection," he answered, anticipating the rest of her question.

He still hadn't turned around to face her. He was trying his best to get himself under control before he did that. There were times, less now than before, when facing Alex was not an easy thing to do, even under the best of circumstances.

This was definitely *not* the best of circumstances. Men weren't supposed to cry. It wasn't anything that had been drummed into him; it was just something that he felt. Most of all, he didn't want Alex to see him with tears in his eyes. So he struggled to get control over himself.

"I'm sorry for your loss."

The words came to her lips automatically—and sounded incredibly tinny and hollow to her ear, even though they were filled to capacity and then some with the truth. She meant them from the bottom of her heart.

"I'm sorry for ours, too," she added in a voice that was even smaller than when she'd begun. "Your father was a wonderful, wonderful man and we're all going to miss him terribly. Especially me."

Wyatt turned from the window then, his face a rigid mask of control. Only the sunlight shining on the slight telltale dampness on his cheek belied the control he was attempting to project.

"You're kidding," he said in disbelief.

Alex had no idea what he was referring to. Had his grief caused him to temporarily take leave of his senses? "What?"

"You're actually engaging in one-upman-ship? Now?" he asked her incredulously.

"What?" Alex repeated, thoroughly confused. Then his words sank in and she stared at him, horrified. How could he even *think* that? "No. I only meant that I was going to miss your father a great deal."

"That's not what you said," Wyatt pointed out. "You said 'especially me.' That means that out of everyone who is griev-ing—including me—*you* are the one who is grieving the most. *You,* who only saw him for a month in the summer and a cou-ple of times during the year, you're going to miss him more than I am."

She refrained from pointing out that he only saw his father the same amount she did. But that would be nit-picking and this was *not* the time for that.

"That's not what I meant. I mean—oh, damn it, Wyatt," she cried in frustration, "I'm trying my best to be nice, here."

"Something you obviously don't have much practice at because you're not suc-ceeding," he told her.

She pulled back, hurt and confused.

"I'm sorry," he said. "Maybe I'm being unreasonable, but I just don't see you making an effort. My dad died last night, and all I see is Alex being…Alex. At my expense."

The next moment, any possible escalation of a verbal exchange between Alex and Dan's son was interrupted as people came flooding into the small office, filling it to capacity.

Cris, Stevi and Andy surrounded Wyatt, offering their condolences in what came across as a cacophony of sympathy and kind words tripping over one another.

Only her father noticed Alex retreating from the room, moving back to the threshold.

"Everything all right?" he asked her.

"No," she answered, forcing herself to tear her eyes away from Wyatt and her sisters. Their comfort was easing his pain. She was glad for him, really glad—but she had tried to do the same thing, she really had. And he had just railed at her. "Uncle Dan's gone," she added in response to what she knew was going to be her father's next question. "How can *anything* be all right at this moment?"

"I meant between you and Wyatt," her father clarified.

"No," she told him honestly. "But then," she added, "it never was." Alex shrugged the matter off. "That's not important right now." She focused on something she *could* help with. "If Uncle Dan just died yesterday, then there hasn't been a funeral yet."

"No, there hasn't," Wyatt said, speaking up. Despite having three women talking to him at once, he had still managed to hone in on what Alex had said to her father.

"That's part of the reason Wyatt's here," her father told her.

Alex was still contemplating ducking out, but with everyone watching that seemed too much like running and it wasn't the kind of message she was looking to send. When she came right down to it, she wasn't sure exactly *what* kind of message she was trying to send.

"To carry out Dan's last wishes," her father was saying. "Dan wanted to be buried here, in the family cemetery. These past twenty years, Ladera-by-the-Sea was really the only place he called home. His summers here with Wyatt and you girls were his haven, it was what he considered both his goal and his reward for a year well lived."

"And Uncle Dan actually said he wanted this to be his final resting place?" Alex asked her father.

Before her father could answer, Wyatt did. "That was what he told me."

That sounded right and fitting somehow, Alex thought. His visits had been the highlight of the summer when she was younger. When he'd suddenly turn up at other times of the year, it always felt like Christmas.

Who was she kidding? Dan *and* Wyatt's visits were both the highlight of her summers, although admittedly for different reasons. Reasons she wasn't about to pick apart right now because she wasn't up to it.

And might never be.

"So we'll hold the services here?" Cris asked her father.

"That's the general idea," Richard replied. He looked at his daughters, each precious to him in her own way. He could see that they were all deeply affected by this. "I think that might help us to say one final goodbye to him."

As usual, Alex instantly began to take charge.

It wasn't so much that she had a need to be in control. It was more that she felt that by picking up the reins, she was allowing everyone else the freedom of doing what they needed to do without having to concern themselves with the bigger-picture details.

"Okay, first off, I'll need a list of people to contact about the funeral services," Alex said to her father.

She knew that the list would be coming from Wyatt, not her father, and this was her way of letting Wyatt know she would be taking care of the arrangements. At this point, she was certain that his state of mind was a shambles. He had trouble accepting what she said during the best of times.

Wyatt surprised her by saying crisply, "Already done."

Wyatt had never been what she had

thought of as organized. But then, maybe he hadn't put the list together. Maybe he had one of those movie starlets she'd seen hanging off his arm each time he attended a premiere of one of the movies he wrote. None of them looked as if she had an IQ rivaling that of a peacock, but obviously one of them probably knew how to write.

"Okay, moving on," Alex announced, shifting her attention to Wyatt. "What date were these people told? For the services that were being held?" she elaborated when she received no answer.

"Day after tomorrow," he finally replied.

Well, that was really quick, she couldn't help thinking. "Pretty confident my father would say yes," Alex said, her eyes locking on to his.

"Why wouldn't he?" he replied, treating her as if she'd just accused him of something. That's not why she'd said it. Something just didn't seem to make sense in this two-day timeline.

"Why wouldn't I?" Her father asked the same question Wyatt had.

"No reason, but the inn could have been

booked solid, making holding the funeral service rather difficult," she pointed out. "Besides, even though the inn *isn't* booked solid, it would have still been nice to have the details nailed down on our end before alerting—how many people were alerted?" she asked, realizing she still didn't have a number to work with.

"My father made friends with the immediate world," Wyatt told her.

"The immediate world," she repeated. "That's going to make for pretty difficult seating arrangements. I'm not sure if we have enough folding chairs for everyone."

"But I cut it down to a hundred," Wyatt continued as if she hadn't said anything. "Is that all right?" he asked, looking at his father's oldest friend.

"Any number you come up with is fine, Wyatt," Richard assured him with feeling. "No matter how many people you want attending the service, we'll find a way to accommodate everyone, so feel free to increase your list if you want to."

But Wyatt shook his head. "No, a hundred's good. But thanks for the offer."

"Well, at least we'll be saving on folding chairs," Alex said, doing her best to keep the situation as light as she could.

If she didn't, Alex was fairly certain she was going to break down in tears herself.

CHAPTER FOUR

"YOU WERE KIND OF sharp with Wyatt back there," Cris commented as she and Alex headed back toward the front of the inn. There was an underlying note of disapproval in her voice. "You could have gone a little easier on him, Alex. After all, the man just lost his father."

"I know. I was there when Dad told us, remember?" Alex said impatiently. "And if I'd suddenly changed and gone completely soft and sweet on him, tiptoeing around his feelings—" she forced a smile to her lips and nodded as they passed one of the inn's recurring guests, Mrs. Rafferty "—Wyatt might have let his guard down—and then who knows what would have happened? This way, he's got his guard up, he knows what to expect and he's too busy trying to block my next barb to let all that pain flatten him."

Cris looked at her older sister, clearly impressed. "So this was actually a 'humanitarian' act on your part?" she asked, trying but failing not to laugh.

Alex could only agree with her: this had to be the most creative excuse for verbally sparring with Wyatt she'd ever come up with.

"Something like that," Alex admitted with a vague, dismissive shrug. She didn't want to harp on the subject, but the truth was, if she'd treated him with kid gloves, Wyatt wouldn't have had the sparring partner he was accustomed to and right now, she had a feeling he needed that. He needed that touch of the familiar to help steady him. "Let's just say that's what I would have wanted if I was in his place."

"Still," Cris pointed out, "a few kind words wouldn't have killed you."

She and Wyatt didn't have that sort of a relationship. Maybe the rules would change sometime down the road—although she really doubted it—but what she did know was that this wasn't the time for change. He needed someone to vent at and right now, for better or worse, that was her.

She cocked her head, as if she was trying to make out something. "I think I hear Ricky calling for his mommy."

Cris shook her head. She had superhearing when it came to her son. "You're impossible, you know that?"

"I'm also older," Alex reminded her with a smile that said she was the one who got to make the rules.

"Next time around, I get to be the older one," Cris declared.

"We'll talk," Alex promised. Rounding the desk, she got back to work.

Alex heard her sister muttering under her breath as she made her way to the kitchen.

The kitchen had, at Cris's insistence, already been updated, upgraded and expanded so she could have elbow room. That included a couple of extra elbows, as well, during their busy season. Elbows attached to people who knew how to take orders and work together when preparing meals became a marathon event rather than the laid-back endeavor it had initially been when Cris had slowly eased herself into the position of the inn's chef.

It's too bad, thought Alex, the contractor who did the kitchen had proved unavailable for their expansion needs. Oh well, she'd find somebody.

With Cris in the kitchen, Dorothy upstairs tending to the bedrooms and their attached baths and her father, Andy and Stevi still back in his office with Wyatt—doing what they could to comfort him in their own way—that left her at the front desk. She was used to holding down the fort but not this ambush of emotions. Wave after wave of sadness kept washing over her, stealing away her heart.

Alex tried to remember the last time she'd seen the man who would soon be laid to eternal rest on the inn's property. It had only been a little more than two weeks ago. She tried to think if she'd actually *looked* at him when they'd talked, or if she'd merely spoken to the image of the man she carried around in her brain.

But as closely as she could recall, Uncle

Dan had seemed perfectly healthy at the time. Oh, maybe he'd seemed a little less robust, but he was all gung ho about what he'd referred to as his next project. She'd thought it strange at the time because he usually referred to his work as assignments, not projects, but she hadn't asked him about it.

Now she wished she had. She wished she'd asked him more questions about his work, spent more time with him. She'd just assumed he'd go on forever, that he had a charmed life. He'd never been so much as wounded in all the years he'd spent covering stories in some of the world's most dangerous hot spots.

Alex remembered one particular postcard he'd sent several years ago. Not to her, exclusively, but to all of them. It was a generic card with his byline logo on the front, and on the back Dan had written, "Miss you all, but *don't* wish you were here. No one sleeps. Everyone's waiting for the next attack to come. Gotta be a better way to earn a living. Love to you all, Uncle Dan."

That was the way he saw himself, she

thought. As their Uncle Dan. It wasn't just a term affixed to parental friends and used strictly by small children. She and her sisters had no other relatives, so she had nothing to compare Dan Taylor to, but if they *had* had an uncle, she knew without hesitation that she would have wanted him to be exactly like the man who had taken to the honorary title without hesitation. Her father had also selected Dan to be her godfather.

They made for strange best friends, her father and Dan. Dan was as vital, as outgoing, as her father was soft-spoken and introverted.

She still couldn't believe that she wouldn't be seeing Dan walk through the inn's tall front doors, bringing in sunlight and blue skies with him.

Alex felt a tear run down her cheek and looked around for something to wipe her eyes with. The box of pop-up tissues on the desk was very pretty and had been chosen because it matched the inn's décor.

It was also very empty.

Frustrated, she tossed the box into the

wastebasket behind the desk and used the back of her hand to wipe the tear away.

As soon as she did, another one slid down her cheek. Followed by a third.

This time, instead of her knuckles, Alex used the heel of her hand. She didn't want to be seen crying by guests.

Besides, this was a private matter and she was a very private person. At bottom, she always had been.

"Why are things never the way they're supposed to be?" she muttered, annoyed over the lack of tissues when she needed them. It was displacement and she knew it, but she used the excuse anyway.

"I don't know, why aren't they?"

Startled—because she'd believed herself to be alone—Alex gasped and swung around.

As she did so, she managed to knock the sign-in ledger onto the floor.

Wyatt bent to pick it up for her and placed the ledger back on the desk.

"You still sneak up on people," Alex accused him, her eyebrows pulling together into a single, exasperated line.

Because it annoyed her—and he desperately needed the diversion—he smiled. "I still have that gift," he confirmed. Seeing the trail of tears on her cheek for the first time, Wyatt reached into his pocket, pulled out a handkerchief and held it out to her. "Here."

She hesitated for a moment, then took the handkerchief gingerly and critically looked over the small, white square.

"Don't worry," Wyatt said, "I only wiped down one bathroom sink with it."

She raised her eyes to his. Oh, come on. She had to know he was being sarcastic. Or, at least he *assumed* she had to know that. Still, she folded the handkerchief so that it was tiny, then used the surface she'd left exposed to slide quickly along her cheeks, drying them.

"Thanks," Alex said, holding the handkerchief out to him again.

"Keep it," he told her, pushing her hand back. "You might need it again."

"No, I won't," she told him firmly. He still made no move to take the handkerchief back. Finally, Alex placed it on the counter and slid it along until it was directly in front of him. She never could let him have the final word.

"So, you figure you've used up your allotted amount of tears and won't be needing that anymore?" he asked, unable to clamp down on his sarcasm.

"No tears," she contradicted him, "just perspiration. And no, I *won't* be needing it again."

"Suit yourself." Reaching into his inside pocket, Wyatt pulled out the handwritten list he'd put together and placed it in front of her. "These are the people I notified about the funeral service. And it's okay to cry, you know," he added out of the blue. "It doesn't make you any less of a person. It might even make you stronger."

Alex laughed dismissively. "That sounds like something you got out of a fortune cookie. You sure you're Uncle Dan's son? He had a fantastic way with words, with creating pictures out of them and getting right to the heart of matters. He put a person right into the thick of the action."

"We have—had…" Wyatt corrected

himself, still struggling to think of his father in anything but the present tense. "We had completely different styles."

Because his father hadn't been around much of the time he'd been growing up, it seemed natural not to see him. Natural to expect to encounter him sometime down the road, but not necessarily right now. Even before the divorce, his father would be gone for weeks, sometimes even a couple of months, at a time. And after the divorce, there were only summers with occasional quick visits in between.

And now, there would be no more visits at all. It wasn't an easy thing to accept. He could feel his heart start to ache all over again. He struggled to rein himself in.

"Dad went to the heart of the action as it was happening. I prefer to study the history of the action and take it apart. Analyze it and find out what led to it. That's why his last project really took me by surprise."

There was that word again. Project. It occurred to Alex that she had no idea what Dan had been working on when he died.

She just assumed—incorrectly it seemed—that it was another piece of war journalism.

"His last project?" she asked Wyatt now, waiting to be enlightened.

Wyatt nodded. "The one he was working on when…when he stopped working."

It was a nice, antiseptic way to say it, wrapping the finality of death in words that implied a temporary break.

It wasn't until Wyatt had said it that way that she realized that was the way she would prefer to deal with Uncle Dan's passing, too. Antiseptically. The other word, the D-word, was far too raw and final for her to utter right now.

Pushing ahead, Alex focused on what Wyatt had begun to say. "What was he working on?"

Wyatt's smile made her feel a little uneasy, although she couldn't have explained why.

"My father was writing a history of the inn."

That wasn't the kind of story Dan usually worked on, she couldn't help thinking. He wrote things that wound up on the front page, or of late, in a blog and sometimes in front of a camera. This sounded as if he was working on a book.

"What inn?" she asked, confused.

Was she serious? Wyatt wondered. So, she hadn't known, either. That seemed rather strange. But then, his father had only told him last week—just before he'd extracted that promise from him.

"This inn."

Alex stared at him. "This isn't some practical joke, is it? Uncle Dan was just here a few weeks ago. He never mentioned this to me.... You're serious?"

"Why wouldn't I be?"

"Because I didn't know anything about it," she snapped.

Ah, he thought. So that's it. She's upset because she knew everything that was going on at the inn at any given time.

And she hadn't known about this.

Of course that would bother her almost as much as his surprising her with a funeral here without any advance warning. No matter what he did and for what reason, he upset her. Always had, and he didn't see a way around it.

"He got all sorts of notes from your father when he got started," Wyatt said, proving just how committed his father had been to the project. "Letters, files, photographs, copies of old ledgers…"

Her jaw dropped.

He hesitated before adding, "If you didn't know about it, maybe it was supposed to be a surprise." All he knew was that his father had asked him to finish it for him, and he'd said the publisher had given him a deadline, which he was to try to keep to.

"A surprise? For whom?" she asked incredulously.

Wyatt said the first thing that occurred to him. "For the rest of you. You and your sisters. I think he envisioned it as a sort of commemorative book on the bed-and-breakfast's 120th anniversary next year."

The exact date was at the end of April. April 27th was the date that Ruth Roman first opened the doors of her home to the public.

Still, Alex thought, there could have been

another reason for undertaking the commemorative book.

"Well, I guess we'll never know now," she said with a sigh.

Wyatt looked at her quizzically. "Why not?"

She looked at him for a long moment. Was he seriously asking her that? No, he was just yanking her chain. But then, she fully expected him to. That was the way Wyatt behaved and right now, it was very important for both of them—not just him but her, as well—to keep normal in sight.

"Well," she began slowly, "I'd say that the obvious reason is because Uncle Dan isn't here to write it anymore."

"He's not," Wyatt agreed, fixing her with his steely gaze, clearly refusing to give in to his emotions, "but I am."

Her eyebrows pulled together as she studied him. "And what's that supposed to mean?"

"I wouldn't have thought I'd have to spell it out for you. But…this has been an…a traumatic day. What it means is that my dad asked me to finish it for him and I said yes."

"You're going to write a book about the inn?" Alex asked even more incredulously.

"Yes," he said. "I have to. I gave my father my word that I would."

"But you write movie scripts and fiction nobody reads." Alex threw in the last part to cover up the fact that she not only knew about his books, she secretly read them, as well. And when she did, she could hear his voice on every page. That was something else she wouldn't admit, along with the fact that she found him to be a good writer, as good a writer in his own way as his father.

But telling Wyatt that would only enlarge his ego and, in her opinion, it was large enough as it was.

"Maybe they'll read this one," he speculated. "Besides, I'm committed." He watched her carefully, anticipating her reaction—and his own amusement to that reaction. "I made the arrangements with Dad's publisher and in order to work within the deadline he'd initially agreed to, I'm going to have to focus exclusively on the book."

He waited for her to say something. When she didn't, he added what he knew would be the salt to her wound.

"I thought it might be easier for me if I just stayed here at the inn while I write it. That way, if there are any questions that come to mind, I can ask one of you about it."

"They've got this great, newfangled invention called the telephone. It lets you call people whenever you want and ask them all the questions in the world," Alex pointed out.

"Not quite the same thing as talking to someone face-to-face."

She couldn't begin to imagine how long it would take him to write a book. The thought of having him around for an extended period of time was incomprehensible to her—not to mention unacceptable.

"How about Skype?" she suggested. "That let's you talk face-to-face."

"More like screen-to-face." he said with obvious relish. He was enjoying this a little too much. Shouldn't he be too deep in his grief to enjoy tormenting her so much? "Besides, staying at the inn might inspire me. It'll talk to me."

"We don't have ghosts here," Alex informed him darkly.

"Maybe not." The smile on his lips was maddening. It was the one he wore when he triumphed over her in anything. "But we do have your dad and your sisters. And you," he added as if it was an afterthought.

"That's because we all *work* here," she said through gritted teeth. "And our busy season is about to start."

"I promise I won't bother you." He even crossed his heart like a ten-year-old girl, which she had to bite her tongue not to tell him. "It'll be as if I was invisible."

Pointing out that he was already bothering her, that the thought of him being here, twenty-four hours a day for who knew how long, *really* bothered her, was something she wasn't prepared to admit. It was hard enough to admit that to herself. She knew him, knew that he'd take that information, turn it inside out and find a way to use it against her in some fashion.

And then, after turning their lives upside down, Wyatt would finish his book, go back to his home in Hollywood, surround himself with women whose IQs probably came in low double digits and laugh about his stay at the quaint inn.

She could feel herself getting annoyed in response even just thinking about it.

"Not invisible enough for me," she explained.

He looked at her for a long moment, wondering exactly when she had transformed from a gangly girl who was all arms and legs—and sharp tongue—into an extremely attractive, nicely proportioned young woman. Although her tongue could still slice through concrete with absolutely no effort at all.

"Well, you look busy so I'll leave you to your work. Let me know if you need anything else from me." He began to back away.

A postcard from the other side of the world comes to mind, she thought, but, in the interest of peace, she kept that to herself.

As Cris had pointed out, the man had just lost his father so she needed to cut him some slack. Later, she promised herself she would take that slack, wrap it around Wyatt's neck and hang him with it. Or at least pull it tight. Very tight.

She found the scenario somewhat comforting.

Dwelling on it took her mind off both Uncle Dan's sudden passing *and* the fact that despite efforts to the contrary, she found herself oddly attracted to a man she wanted desperately to dismiss and wipe from her memory.

Alex pressed her lips together and looked at the list of names. She had work to do now, no time for anything else.

They were going to need verbal confirmations, and quickly, from all these people so she could tell Cris how much food she needed to order for the reception they were going to hold right after the funeral service.

Exhaling a breath, Alex threw herself into her work.

CHAPTER FIVE

ALEX FELT LIKE the last air-traffic controller left in the tower with a dozen planes circling the field in a holding pattern. She was almost too busy to breathe.

The funeral was less than two days away, but from all the phone calls she'd made, she gleaned that people would begin arriving tomorrow morning and continue arriving throughout the day. For most, their first stop would be the inn, to touch base with Wyatt and to decide just where they would be staying until after the funeral.

Every available room she had left was quickly booked. That was the easy part. The hard part was going to be deciding which hotel in the area would be the most suitable as well as the most affordable for the rest of the mourners who were coming. She didn't want to just toss out hotel names and addresses at them. That seemed grossly insensitive to her. Alex wanted to be able to make proper recommendations to these people who were coming to pay their last respects to the man she and her family had loved so dearly.

Which was why she was still up way past her usual eleven o'clock bedtime, going over the particulars she'd gathered from all the phone calls she'd made.

"But why go through all that trouble?" Andy asked, looking at all the work she was putting in.

Alex had just busted her baby sister as the latter was attempting to sneak into the inn and up to her room without being seen.

While Andy was twenty years old, their father liked her in relatively early on a weeknight. And that so-called curfew was long past. Andy had just promised to become her personal slave if she didn't tell on her. It wasn't that Andy was afraid of any sort of punishment from their father, she just didn't want to see the disappointed look in his eyes, and especially not when he was trying to deal with the loss of his best friend.

"Why bother? Because *I'm* not giving my seal of approval, Andy, the inn is. That's how the people attending Uncle Dan's funeral will remember it, especially if they're overcharged or unhappy with the service they get at the hotel *I* told them to go to. I don't want the inn getting a black mark because I just assumed all the hotels around here take as much care to keep their guests happy as we do."

Andy leaned against the reception desk, shaking her head. "Alex, do you ever go off duty and just think of you, not the inn?"

"Sure I do. Lots of times," Alex answered a bit too quickly, then waved her sister off. "Now go upstairs before Dad comes down for a midnight snack and finds you trying to sneak in."

Andy nodded, beginning to leave. She stopped and looked over her shoulder. "You *do* know he's being way overprotective, right?"

Alex laughed softly. Andy wasn't experiencing anything that the rest of them hadn't gone through at her age. But this time around, she supposed that her father was being slightly more intense because after Andy, there were no more daughters to fuss over.

"You're his little girl, Andy, the last of the bunch." She grinned. "Knowing Dad, he'll probably go with you on your honeymoon, just to make sure your new husband's treating you right."

Andy rolled her eyes. A noise coming from the rear of the inn made her jump, curtailing any further discussion. "Gotta go!" she declared in a hoarse whisper.

And then Andy made good her getaway, hurrying up the stairs before she was caught.

Probably just the cat, Alex thought as she went back to searching through several websites she'd discovered that listed people's reactions to their stays at one or another of the local hotels. Some had even extensively cited their likes and dislikes. Alex made a few notes to herself on the pad she kept by the computer.

"Don't you ever go to bed?"

Startled, Alex felt her heart slam against her rib cage.

Obviously, it wasn't the cat rattling around, making noise.

She really wished it had been.

She forced herself to look up slowly, giving herself a second to bank down any telltale sign that he'd startled her.

"On occasion," Alex replied. "Most of the time I just hang upside down in a cave." She guessed that Wyatt was probably thinking something along those lines.

He laughed shortly. "You'll have to let me watch sometime." He rounded the desk and dropped into the chair beside it.

"Sometime," she echoed, deliberately making her answer vague.

He saw the computer. It was on the shelf beneath the counter. Alex had obviously gone out of her way to keep the iconic symbol of progress out of the immediate line of sight because it simply did *not* go with the Victorian décor.

Curious to see what she was searching at this hour—it never occurred to him that she might be doing something strictly for pleasure—Wyatt moved his chair closer so that he could get a better look at the monitor.

Since when did she concern herself with other hotels? he wondered.

"What are you doing?" he asked, nodding at the computer screen.

Her answer wasn't really enlightening. "I'm checking out nearby hotel accommodations."

Getting information out of her had never been easy—unless she was taunting him with it, he recalled, thinking back to one particularly miserable summer when he was thirteen and she was almost twelve—and temporarily taller than he was.

"Thinking of running away?" he asked mildly. "Or are you suddenly changing allegiance?"

"Neither," she informed him crisply. "I'm anticipating that the people coming for the funeral will need a place to stay and if they ask, I need to have something concrete *and* worthwhile to recommend."

She noticed the somewhat bemused expression on his face. Now what was *that* supposed to mean? The man was *so* hard to read. Not for the first time, she thought that he should have come with some sort of a "how-to" instruction manual. Or, at the very least, a booklet with informative pictures, like for a piece of furniture that had to be put together.

Alex took a guess as to what was on his mind. In this case, it wasn't exactly difficult. "What, you thought we'd put them all up here? In case it slipped your mind with all those parties you're always attending with your Hollywood friends, the inn only has twenty-three rooms and half of those are filled right now. I wound up booking the first few people I called on your list so there're no longer any vacancies here. There's no way we could take in all the mourners, even if they were willing to double up. They certainly wouldn't want to *quadruple* up or even more." When Wyatt didn't say anything to agree with her or comment on what she'd said, she continued. "I'm assuming that these aren't all college freshmen coming to the service."

"They're friends of my dad's," Wyatt responded. "Journalists, for the most part. I know for a fact that at least half of them are used to roughing it."

"Which means that half of them aren't." She wasn't about to put anyone out or to inconvenience a single person who was coming to honor Uncle Dan. "Besides, I'm assuming that those who have one are bringing their spouses. Our rooms are bigger than old-fashioned phone booths, but we're certainly not going to see how many people we can cram into them."

As she talked, Alex continued perusing the sites, scanning over guests' comments and criticisms, as well as what they found praiseworthy. She meant to take care of all the people coming to the funeral. It was the least she could do for Uncle Dan.

"You know, I don't remember you being this conscientious when we were growing up," Wyatt commented. The remark was meant to hide the fact that he thought she was going out of her way to do a very nice thing and he appreciated it. He knew it was rather juvenile, but he wasn't comfortable praising her.

Alex blew out a dismissive breath. "I'm surprised that you remember anything at all about the summers you spent here."

"On the contrary, I remember a lot," he assured her. "Why would you think I wouldn't remember anything?"

Alex shrugged. "You live in Hollywood, land of the well-endowed and the implanted."

When she said nothing further, Wyatt could only stare at her. Was that some kind of code he was supposed to decipher? Well-endowed? "Still not an answer to my question."

"Well, that's the only answer you're going to get from me right now." If she said something more about the well-endowed women she'd seen pictured with him, Wyatt might misunderstand and think she was being jealous, or something equally as absurd.

She was overly tired and that made her careless, she realized. Too careless.

Alex powered down her computer, knowing she wasn't going to get any more work done tonight. Besides, she had enough information to make an intelligent recommendation to the mourners.

The screen winked at her, then shut down, and she rose to her feet.

About to say good-night, she saw by his expression that he was momentarily preoccupied, as if a thought had sneaked up on him.

Debating just leaving him to that thought, she found she couldn't. What if he was thinking about how lonely the inn seemed without his father around? The two had always been here together and while there were more than a few times when Uncle Dan would just visit them on his own, Wyatt had *never* been here before without his father.

Except that now he was.

It really had to feel strange.

Her heart went out to him.

"How are you holding up?" Alex asked him quietly.

Her voice was barely above a whisper, but he heard her anyway. Looking up, his eyes met hers. The smile that came to his lips was enigmatic.

"I'm doing okay," he said, and she took that as her release from any further obligation, at least for tonight. He said he was fine, she told herself, so she was free to leave him alone.

But as she started to go, Wyatt added, "As long as I don't think about why I'm here or what I'm doing." He sighed quietly. "Or about the fact that I can't see him anymore, can't pick up the phone and talk to him—well, actually, I couldn't do that even when he was...even before," he amended, unable to say "alive," the word that no longer applied to his father and so permanently separated them. "I'd leave him a message that I wanted to talk to him and he'd call me back. Usually the same day."

Wyatt smiled to himself. "Half the time he'd call back in the middle of the night, because he'd forget about the time difference until I'd answer the phone, half asleep." He looked out through the large bay window that faced the front of the inn. The darkness beyond effectively hid the grounds, intensifying a feeling of isolation, of being separated from the rest of the world. "I'm going to miss him," he all but whispered.

"We're all going to miss him," Alex assured him with feeling.

It wasn't the same thing. "Yeah, but you're going to miss your father's friend— I'm going to miss my *father,*" he emphasized. "Miss having the adult relationship I was looking forward to having with him." And then he shrugged, remembering who he was talking to. "I guess that probably doesn't make any sense to you."

She surprised him by saying, "On the contrary, that makes perfect sense to me."

Wyatt stared at her. He hadn't expected Alex to be this intuitive, this sensitive to his feelings. He found himself waiting for a shoe to drop—or an ax to fall.

"I lost my mother," she reminded him. She didn't expect him to remember any details about her. His life, since they were kids, had gotten very complicated—as well as filled with glamorous women. "I know exactly how you feel."

Their eyes met as he rose to his feet.

Somehow they'd ended up standing just inches apart.

"Maybe you do, at that," he agreed, knowing how very close she was to her family.

For a moment the air seemed to stand still between them. Alex suddenly felt this irresistible urge to comfort him, to brush her lips along his cheek and tell him it was all going to be all right, but it was going to take time. A great deal of time.

The intimacy of her thoughts, of her feelings, took her aback.

Alex deliberately looked at her watch. "How about that? We must have set some kind of a record."

Wyatt arched an eyebrow. He wasn't following her. "A record?"

Alex nodded. "We've been talking for fifteen minutes and haven't gotten into an argument yet."

He laughed, then, realizing she was right. "I'd better leave then, before the moment is ruined," he said, amusement playing along his lips.

She nodded, doing her best to look as if she was serious. "Good idea."

"More agreement. This *is* some kind of record," Wyatt mused. "Too bad my dad's not around to see it."

Alex ached for his loss—and for her own. She pressed her lips together and then nodded. "Yes, too bad," she echoed sadly.

After the fact, Wyatt wasn't sure just what came over him. A wave of gratitude, no doubt.

Leaning forward, he placed his hand on her shoulder and lightly brushed his lips against hers before murmuring, "Thanks."

With that, he left.

As he walked away, Wyatt was surprised by the lingering sweetness he could taste on his lips.

Maybe the loss of his father so suddenly *was* devastating him, after all, he thought, quickening his pace just a little.

He needed to get a grip.

Alex remained where she was, watching him walk away, trying to make sense of and sort out just what had taken place here.

He'd kissed her.

Not on a dare, the way he said he had all those years ago when they were kids. Back then he'd caught her by surprise, too, making her pulse race and setting her imagination into high gear.

To cover up her reaction, she'd demanded to know what he thought he was doing. That was when he'd told her he'd kissed her on a dare.

She'd pushed him into the lake.

And then she'd been angry, hurt and annoyed with herself for even entertaining any sort of adolescent romantic thoughts of him. She'd vowed to go to her grave hating him—and promising herself to exact revenge before that occurred.

As an adult, she still thought of that kiss and her humiliation on occasion. And, as an adult, she often wondered if his confession that it had been a dare was the truth or…something that had never occurred to her as a child…was a lie he'd told to cover up his attraction to her and his momentary slip.

She slowly slid her tongue along her lips and tasted him.

They weren't kids anymore.

Maybe they were both just overly tired, overly devastated by the loss of someone who had been important to both of them in different ways.

Survivors of a natural disaster tended to band together for solace, she reminded herself. Seeking comfort in one another.

Temporarily.

Once a routine was struck again, and the loss assimilated and made part of the fabric of their everyday lives, things would get back to normal.

And things would get back to normal for them, as well, she thought. Which meant that she and Wyatt would go back to being friendly adversaries, or frenemies, or whatever the popular term for what she and Wyatt were these days.

Before she could think to stop herself, Alex realized that she was running the tip of her tongue along the outline of her lips again.

Feeling the firm, fleeting imprint of his lips.

Feeling her heart skip a beat as it searched for a path back to normal.

She turned down the light in the reception area until there was just a soft, dim ambience cast over the area. A person who was exhausted tended to magnify everything. That was why she'd reacted to Wyatt the way she just had.

Her feelings weren't in that kiss, just her sympathies.

Served her right for staying up so late.

You've got to get an early start in the morning and you've gotta be fresh, not just for all those people you know are coming but there're all those funeral arrangements to still take care of.

Wyatt, she had already established, had taken care of the basics. If they were going to do right by Uncle Dan, though, there were a lot of details she still needed to handle, beginning with securing a minister to preside over the services and the actual burial.

"You're going to have company, Mom," she murmured, as she made her way to her room. "Remember Uncle Dan? You married Dad at the same time that Uncle Dan married his wife. You and Dad did a whole lot better than Uncle Dan and Elizabeth did." Reaching her room, she unlocked her door and went in.

She refrained from turning on any lights. There was a full moon out and moonlight was streaming into her room with a vengeance.

Alex stood there for a moment, just absorbing the peacefulness.

"You won't be so lonely anymore," she promised with a small, sad smile. "Uncle Dan will make you laugh, Mom. He could always make anyone laugh, no matter how grim they were. Be sure to take good care of him, Mom. Show him the ropes. He'll catch on quick."

Her eyes filled with tears, tears she struggled not to shed. It was a struggle she was destined to lose and she knew it.

Alex unbuttoned her blouse and stepped out of her skirt. Ordinarily she was exceedingly neat and would hang up her clothes, but tonight, she was far too exhausted to care about being neat.

Too exhausted to even try to remember which drawer had her nightgown in it.

Instead, she just slipped into bed still in her underwear. It had been one exhaustingly long day.

Alex was asleep within two minutes.

CHAPTER SIX

ALEX HAD EVERY intention of getting up at 6:00 a.m., if not before. So when she turned on her side and looked at her alarm clock, the blue digital numbers didn't register at first.

And then they did.

Six thirty-two.

Alex bolted upright. She'd overslept!

Five seconds later she hit the ground running. Her inner alarm had failed her, most likely because she had too many different things going on in her head at the same time, but even so, the excuse was unacceptable to her. There was just too much for her to do to waste time sleeping.

Her shower took all of three minutes. Washing and drying her hair took another nine. Her body was still damp when she hurried into her clothes, getting stuck in them in her haste, causing her temper to fray.

She *should* have set the alarm, Alex upbraided herself. But the truth of it was, she hated hearing the alarm go off, vibrating into her consciousness—even if it wasn't shrill. She hated the sound so much that she'd trained her brain to wake her moments before she was supposed to actually get up.

Ordinarily, that worked.

But then, these were not exactly ordinary circumstances. Alex slipped her feet into her favorite pair of high heels. For one thing, between today and tomorrow, the inn was going to be inundated with people, coming and going. For another, this was the first funeral to be held on the premises in a long time.

The first, she thought, since her mother had been laid to rest.

Alex paused to check herself in the mirror and then hurried out of her room.

The inn was better suited to weddings, she thought. She'd witnessed several here in the past few years—couples found the

Victorian veranda hopelessly romantic as a backdrop as they exchanged their vows. They also loved the way the inn looked in the background in their wedding photographs.

But a funeral, well, that was something entirely different.

Granted, there had been funerals here, but for the life of her, she couldn't even remember the service for her mother's. She had somehow completely blocked it out of her memory.

Consequently, she was flying blind, making all the different arrangements on her own. She could have asked her father for help, but she was determined to take care of this for him, to allow him to do whatever he needed to, to begin his own healing process.

So, Alex did what she always did when she attacked something new—or when there were just too many varying components at play for her to keep track of. She made lists. Lists of everything to be addressed before the actual service and subsequent burial took place. Lists of what to do *after* the burial.

Lists that begat lists.

She'd started making the first list last night. And now, as she began to go through her paces—fortified with a large mug of coffee Dorothy had thought to bring her— it seemed to her that for every task she checked off, two more things that needed doing occurred to her. Alex dutifully added them at the end of the list.

In her mind, she'd already dubbed it the List Without End and was doing her level best not to let it overwhelm her.

She'd been at it for an hour when her father came to the reception desk.

"I thought I'd find you here," he said. He noted the near-empty mug. "Have you had breakfast yet?"

"Later," she told him. "I've got to catch up. I got a late start," she confessed.

"How late?" he asked.

"I woke up at six-thirty," she answered ruefully as she double-checked something near the bottom of her list.

"Six-thirty," her father repeated, shaking his head. "Only you." Richard placed his hand over hers, stilling her for a moment. "Nobody expects you to juggle this by yourself, Alex. I appreciate you taking charge of the arrangements, but this is still my inn and I should really be the one taking care of my best friend's funeral, not you."

She wasn't about to argue with him—but she wasn't about to listen, either. Like her sisters, she was very protective of her father. Unlike them, she'd had a great deal of practice at it.

"You just take care of yourself, Dad," she told him, moving her hand from beneath his and giving his hand a squeeze, then returned to typing on the keyboard. "And if you really want to do something for me—"

"Yes?" he asked.

"Run interference with Wyatt for me. He's bound to have some questions or suggestions and I'd appreciate it if you handled that for me."

After last night, she wasn't sure if she was all that comfortable dealing with Wyatt just yet. She still wasn't sure what to make of the kiss—that included understanding why he had done it or admitting to herself how she felt about being on the receiving end.

"That shouldn't be too hard for you since the two of you have such a special relationship, anyway," she added.

Her father looked closely at her, appearing more than a little perplexed. "I'm not sure I understand what you mean, Alex."

He was trying to spare her feelings, she supposed. But there was no point in that. She'd long since come to terms with the situation.

"Dad, it's okay," she told him with a sincere smile. "I get it, I understand."

"Well, that makes one of us," he said, appearing more confused, not less. "I think I might need subtitles to know what you're getting at. Just what do you mean by 'special relationship' and just what is it that you 'understand'?"

Why was her father putting her through this? She was telling him she understood his need for a son and that it was okay with her that he'd fulfilled that need with Wyatt, even though, at bottom, it really wasn't. The little girl she had once been was still very hurt, but she was doing her best not to let him see that. Just what more did he want from her?

"Well, Wyatt's a guy."

"I think we can all agree on that," Richard said slowly.

Did he think she was that thick? The clues had always been there. A mentally challenged raccoon could have figured it out. "Dad, you call all four of us by guys' nicknames."

"Yes?" The single word urged her to continue.

Alex sighed. She didn't have time for this. But her father gave no indication of budging until this was laid out in the open for him. So be it. "Dad, it's obvious."

"Possibly," he granted, then added, "but it's not obvious to me."

Okay, she would spell it all out, every single letter. "Wyatt's the son you never had but always wanted. Whenever Uncle Dan arrived with him, you lit up like a Christmas tree. And I heard you that time."

"Heard me?" he asked.

She let out a sigh. She did *not* want to sound as if she was accusing him of anything, but she was at a loss as to how to say this *without* sounding as if she was. "I heard you tell Uncle Dan that he didn't know how very lucky he was to have a son to do things with."

For a moment he just continued to look at her—and then enlightenment struck. "I said that to him when he was lamenting that he wasn't equipped to be a father, that he thought he'd wind up failing Wyatt. I pointed out the plusses to him to make him see that he *was* equal to the job."

He could see that she still wasn't convinced, so he tried again. "And I lit up, as you call it, because I was glad to see my best friend and that he'd lucked out again, defying the odds and staying alive despite the fact that he went to some of the most dangerous hellholes on the planet."

"And Wyatt had nothing to do with the way you reacted when he and Uncle Dan first arrived each summer?" she asked, studying his face for any signs of contradiction.

"Only insofar as the fact that Wyatt was his son and I wanted them both to have a good time while they were here at my inn. But it was catching up with Dan that I looked forward to," he insisted. "If you recall, I used to urge Wyatt to go join you and your sisters."

"I…remember."

He refrained from saying that this very fact made his point. If he'd doted on his best friend's son, he would have kept him around. Taken him out fishing, or some other father-and-son cliché outings. "And?"

She shrugged awkwardly. "I thought you made him hang around us because you wanted me to be more like him."

The sideways thinking of his ordinarily perceptive daughter astounded him. "Granted, Wyatt was a great kid, but so were you. Except, of course, when the two of you got together," he said, vividly remembering incident after incident when they had gone at each other, bickering incessantly, each trying to embarrass the other. He had thought they were never going to survive that. At least now he was beginning to understand why Alex always seemed to instigate fights. "Back then it was like throwing a lit match into a stream of gasoline—instant explosions."

Why hadn't he recognized what was behind their antagonism earlier? He'd tried so hard to be a good father to his girls, but he hadn't seen past his daughter's actions to understand what had caused her to act out against his best friend's son.

She'd been insecure in his love for her.

Well, he'd have to make that up to her. Somehow.

Alex shook her head, amazed by what she was being told. Had she been wrong all this time? Jealous of Wyatt when there was no reason to be? "I always thought you liked Wyatt more than you liked me."

"And here I thought you were the smart one," Richard said, reaching out for her and taking her in his arms. He hugged her and kissed the top of her head before stepping back. "Now, then, is that one of your famous lists?" he asked, his voice suddenly gruff. He nodded at the paper she had on the counter in front of her. It was covered with entries, not all of which were legible.

"It's one of them," she confirmed.

"One of them," Richard repeated in disbelief. "Alex, you do realize this is just a simple funeral for an old friend, not the second invasion of Normandy."

"The absence of gunfire gave me my first clue," she replied. She glanced at her watch, noting that she had already used up too much time. Time she didn't have to spare. "Now, will you take care of Wyatt for me?"

"Why do I need to be taken care of?" Wyatt asked, coming up behind her. "'Morning, Uncle Rick. Alex." He nodded at each of them as he approached the desk where he and Alex had shared a moment last night.

"You have *got* to get squeaky shoes," Alex growled, annoyed that Wyatt had managed to catch her off guard again. If he kept this up, her nerves would be stripped down to nubs by the time the service took place tomorrow.

"Why? It's fun to watch you grow pale and then return to normal again," Wyatt explained. "It's better than a magic act."

Alex ignored his response. "As for why you need to be taken care of, what I meant by that is that I thought my father should help keep you occupied, entertained, if you will. You shouldn't have to *do* anything except show up tomorrow for the service and reception."

"He was my father," Wyatt pointed out, as if that would explain something to Alex.

"And we all loved him," she responded with feeling.

"And because we did," her father interrupted, "we want to set his son's mind at ease and handle all the details regarding the funeral so that he—meaning you—doesn't have to."

"If it's all the same to you," Wyatt began patiently because he intended to remain calm around his father's friend, "I don't *want* to have all the details handled. I want to be the one handling at least some of them." He could tell by Alex's expression that this wasn't being received well. "Look, it's not that I don't appreciate the help," he told her. "I do. But I want to be involved in this. I *need* to be involved in this."

"If you have one weakness, Alex," her father chimed in gently, "it's that you don't delegate."

She gave him a significant look, remembering Christmas dinners that were late when she was a child because her father was helping a guest, or dealing with some aspect or other of the inn's business.

"I wonder where I get it from," she said, looking at him pointedly.

Richard pretended not to understand what she was referring to. "Never mind that, now. From the looks of it, that 'to do' list of yours has given birth to several offspring and we can all pitch in to pare that down." He put his hand out, waiting.

Her father was right. She did have a problem delegating, but she knew she had to. Otherwise, her tendency to handle everything herself was going to make her obsessive.

"Well, I've already called all the people on the list that Wyatt gave me," she told her father. "And everyone on it said they were coming." She produced a second list from inside the reception desk where she'd left it last night. "I was going to call in the additional food order to our suppliers this morning."

Her father took that list from her. "Cris can do that. She's the one who'll be preparing the food for the reception."

"Speaking of which," she said, "Cris is going to need help."

He didn't question her. The length of the list of attending guests was convincing. "All right, I'll handle that."

"You're going to cook?" Alex asked incredulously, staring at him.

"No, I meant I'll find Cris some help. I'll ask Dorothy to give her a hand. She took over the kitchen when Cris went to Disneyland with Ricky and Andy for a few days last year, remember?"

What Alex predominantly remembered was having to take over when Dorothy had become overwhelmed with having to prepare several meals at the same time. Dorothy was a good cook, but she wasn't a fast one.

Alex had another solution. "Tell you what, Dad, why don't you call Rosemary and have her help Cris?" she suggested.

Rosemary King was a longtime friend of the family. Actually, the woman had been her mother's friend first. Her *best* friend. After Rosemary's husband had passed away, she'd bought a modest home not that far from the inn and dropped by periodically. The habit continued even after her mother had died.

Alex and her sisters were fairly convinced that over time, the woman had developed feelings for their father. He, in typical male fashion, was utterly oblivious of this particular development.

Maybe something could be done to help that along a little, Alex thought. And what better time than the present?

"Rosemary?" her father asked as if he hadn't heard the name before.

"Yes, Rosemary," Alex repeated. "She's a whiz in the kitchen, in case you never noticed." Then, anticipating his giving her an argument, Alex reminded him, "You said to delegate."

Richard inclined his head, conceding the point. "All right, I'll give her a call."

"And what do you have in mind for me?" Wyatt asked.

His question caused last night to flash through her mind in vivid detail. The memory brought with it a wave of heat.

It took Alex a moment to rise above both, as she struggled to collect herself.

"Well, if you insist on being involved—"

"I do."

"—you can help me direct your father's friends to the hotel where they'll be staying. Unless, of course, they've already booked arrangements before they left." She saw her father stop walking away and look in her direction. Alex knew what he was going to ask before he asked it. "I thought they might like to go to the Fairmont. The hotel is close by, reasonably priced and I've already checked to see if they have enough rooms to handle this crowd." She inclined her head as she answered that question, too. "They do."

"The Fairmont," her father repeated. She knew he was familiar with the hotel, having told the girls countless times how he'd watched it being constructed when he was a teenager. It had a good reputation. "Good choice. I'll call their reservations desk to alert them of the—"

"Already done," she said. "I sent them an email last night, asking if they could accommodate overflow—eleven of the people coming to the funeral are going to be staying here at the inn," she added. "The Fairmont sent back a confirmation first thing this morning, saying they would be more than happy to put them up." Out of the corner of her eye, she saw Wyatt looking at her, an amused expression on his face. "What?"

"Nothing," he said. "I was just thinking that you really seem to know how to get things moving once you set your mind to it."

"And this surprises you." It was more of a statement than a question.

She almost missed seeing her father smile.

"Not really," Wyatt admitted somewhat reluctantly. "My dad used to talk about how he didn't know how your dad did it, raising four daughters all by himself, each one more capable than the next. He sang your praises a lot, referring to you as a dynamo. I think he was a little envious of you, Uncle Rick."

Alex's father laughed at the comment. "I guess the grass is always greener on the other side."

"You *were* envious of him," Alex concluded. She was right, after all. Her father *did* envy Uncle Dan for having a son.

"Not of him, exactly," Richard amended, "but I have to admit there were times when I wondered what it would be like just to pick up and follow the latest breaking story, living by my wits and out of a suitcase, instead of making sure each bedroom had enough fresh linens."

"Don't forget to add dodging bullets," Alex deliberately pointed out.

"Yes, there's that, too," Richard conceded. "I guess, all things considered, I was better off right here, putting up with raised voices and tantrums instead of bullets."

"Don't know what you're talking about," Alex responded, as if she had no memory of just how very loud and lively she and her sisters could get. "We were all angels. Well, maybe not Stevi. But she grew out of it—just last week." She winked at Wyatt.

"I'll be sure to let her know that," Richard said with a wide smile.

Her mission was accomplished, at least this part of it, Alex told herself. She'd finally gotten her father to smile and to focus on something other than this loss that had ambushed him. She knew that it wasn't over, but each day would get a sliver better and a tiny bit easier.

"Go call Rosemary," she instructed, waving him off.

"I'm on it," he announced, retreating just as the front door opened.

Wyatt turned toward the entrance as an older couple walked in.

"Looks like I'm on, as well," he said to Alex. The next moment, he came around the front desk to greet the first arrivals.

CHAPTER SEVEN

"I DON'T KNOW if I can do this, Alex," Cris said as she let in yet another deliveryman through the rear entrance of the kitchen. This one was bringing in several cartons of assorted vegetables. "According to the head count you gave me, there're going to be over a hundred people attending the reception. Maybe close to twice that if they all bring someone with them. That's two hundred people. I've never cooked for more than twenty people at any one time."

"I know," Alex told her. "Which is why I got you help."

"Why couldn't Wyatt have just stuck to the traditional funeral fare? Everybody loves little sandwiches with the crusts cut off—egg salad and tuna? Who doesn't love that?"

Alex took her sister by the shoulders and

looked her in the eye. "Calm down, Cris. Deep breaths."

"All I'm saying is…" Cris paused to inhale and exhale. "Squares and tarts are expected at funerals. Why do we need to serve a full buffet meal?"

"These guests are coming from all over the place," Alex explained. "Wyatt thought—and I agree—a meal would give them a chance to visit with like-minded people who each share a love for Dan. A tea just…doesn't seem enough."

Cris nodded slowly, and Alex let her go. The delivery guy was standing impatiently at the door, holding out a clipboard. Chris shook off her brief meltdown and went to see what he needed.

The steady stream of Dan's friends had temporarily abated. Alex had left Wyatt manning the reception desk. She would have really preferred leaving Stevi, but the latter seemed to be AWOL at the moment, so she'd had no choice.

Ordinarily there would have been no need to have someone in constant attendance at the desk, but again, there was nothing ordinary about this situation. Wyatt was admittedly better equipped than she was to handle the people who were coming in. After all, they were his father's associates and friends. He had to know at least some of those people by sight. Besides, the man could be charming when he wanted to be, despite the somber occasion.

She'd left him with a stack of maps and directions she'd printed up on how to get from the inn to the Fairmont Hotel—and back again for tomorrow's service. There were also directions on how to get to the funeral parlor for a viewing later on today.

If there were other questions, questions he couldn't answer, she'd be back within fifteen minutes, if not sooner.

He'd nodded, saying something about trying not to miss her while she was gone.

In some ways, it felt as if nothing had changed and that this was just like any other summer they'd spent at the inn.

Except that it wasn't.

Cris signed the bottom of the greengrocer's invoice. "You got someone to help out tomorrow? Who?" she asked.

Alex was aware that "help" wasn't always that. She was quick to reassure her sister. "I told Dad to call Rosemary. You know she'd be happy to pitch in anytime." She saw the pensive look on Cris's face and guessed what was on her sister's mind. Cris liked to complain that she didn't have any help, but in actuality she was very possessive of her kitchen and didn't exactly welcome intruders with open arms. "It was either her or Dad."

"Dad?" Cris cried, looking around her well-ordered, organized workstations. Her father was more like the proverbial bull in a china shop. "'Helping'? In my kitchen?"

"He thinks it's *his* kitchen," Alex reminded her. After all, it was part of *his* inn. "And technically, he's right. But he needs to be at the funeral, not preparing everything that goes with the buffet we've planned. Besides," she speculated, "I think Rosemary needs to get out more. She's had a crush on Dad for years and I think it's high time we help it along."

Cris stared at her. "What? She has a crush on Dad? Really?"

"You really do need to get out of the kitchen more," Alex told her with a laugh. "And who knows, if Rosemary is around more, maybe this'll be the beginning of something."

Cris double-checked the items in the cartons that had been delivered, making sure she had everything she'd ordered.

"Or the end of it," she murmured.

Alex shook her head. "I keep forgetting what an optimist you are," she said dryly. She looked around the area. "By the way, where's Ricky?"

"Stevi took him to the park for me. They should be there for a good part of the day. I'll be able to get a head start on tomorrow's menu."

Alex detected a weary note in her sister's voice. There was still an incredible amount of things to do. "Hang in there, Cris. This'll all turn out well in the long run," she promised.

Cris looked up at her. There were three inches separating them, not to mention that she was in flats while her sister was wear-

ing high heels. "Except for Uncle Dan,"
she said quietly.

Alex frowned. She didn't want to seem
callous, but she was trying very hard not
to think about the man's passing because
she still felt unequal to the task. She didn't
really want to open the doors to that reality until it became more manageable and
less like falling into a huge, dark, bottom-
less abyss.

"Yeah," she said equally quietly, "except
for that."

Cris went over to the freezer, to see if she
had the right number of mini croissants for
the sandwiches, placing that tray next to a
tray of mozzarella and tomato salads. "Do
you ever think about it, Alex?"

Cris asked the question so absently, she'd
almost missed it. "Think about what?"

Cris turned around to look at her. "You
know, dying."

She could honestly say she'd never con-
templated it.

"I'm usually too busy just trying to make
it to the end of the day to think about that."
She looked more closely at Cris, wonder-

ing what was going on in her sister's head. "Why, do you think about it?"

"I've got a son to worry about," Cris reminded her. "So, yes, I think about it, about not being around for Ricky." She blew out a long, soulful breath. "It kind of comes with the territory."

Alex didn't see the problem. "It's not as if you're alone, you know. If anything, heaven forbid, ever happened to you, there are still three of us here for Ricky, not counting Dad. Your four-year-old will be *well* taken care of. If that's keeping you up at night, you can stop worrying. Consider the situation handled."

Cris shook her head. "No, that's *not* my only concern, Alex."

She could tell by the tone of Cris's voice that this sudden, unexpected intrusion of death as a guest at their inn had started her sister thinking.

"Okay, out with it, Cris. What's bothering you? Tell me," she coaxed when Cris hesitated.

Cris took a deep breath. "I don't want to die before I find love again."

Alex blinked. "As in, with a guy?" she asked a little uncertainly.

"Well, yes, of course as in with a guy. I already know you and the others love me, but it's not the same thing."

Cris was gorgeous—all she had to do was to go out and socialize. There'd be guys all over her in a heartbeat. It wasn't as if they lived at the end of the world, or on an island where men were scarce. The supply here was *definitely* not limited. And, unlike her, Cris was outgoing.

Alex was the one who had a fear of putting herself out there and getting hurt. Which was why she chose not to risk it at all and just bury herself in work. She didn't even have one serious relationship to look back on.

Cris had been married and had a family. The idea that she was afraid of never finding love came as totally unexpected to Alex.

"No," Alex agreed. "At least we'll stick by you."

Cris frowned. "If you're referring to what happened between Tom and me—"

"I am," Alex confirmed without as much as a pause. After Mike had been killed, her sister had gone through a very difficult time. For a very short while, she'd dated someone she'd known in high school. Or rather, someone she'd *thought* she'd known in high school. It hadn't exactly turned out well.

Cris shrugged dismissively. "We just weren't right for each other."

Alex nodded. "Mainly because he had such a short attention span, getting distracted by any female under thirty with a pulse."

"That was Tom, but they're not all like that," Cris protested. She turned her attention back to that night's dinner.

"Thank heaven for small favors," Alex responded with feeling.

"After all, I found Mike and he was terrific. There have to be other guys like that out there."

Cris was right, but this was one of those things that came under the heading of having to kiss a lot of frogs before finding a prince.

"Remember what Mom used to say? If it's meant to happen, it will. In the meantime, this reception is supposed to happen and we need to start nailing down a few key details. The service is at eleven, followed by the reception at twelve-thirty. What do you think?" she asked. "Will you be able to pull this together in time, with the help from Rosemary?"

"You know, that seems like I've got more than enough time, now that my head is clear. Hmm. Maybe I won't need the extra help, after all."

"You'll need the help," Alex said without blinking. "Also, about tomorrow, I've got Andy watching Ricky for you while you and Rosemary get all this together, and Stevi's taking care of the music."

"Music?"

Alex nodded. "Music soothes and all that. It was Uncle Dan who'd bought the keyboard for Stevi and encouraged her to learn how to play in the first place."

Cris nodded, remembering. "I'm really going to miss his visits," she confided sadly.

"Yeah, me, too. It was almost as if he officially ushered in summer with him. It'll be hard separating the two."

"How's Dad holding up?" Cris suddenly asked, taking out spices. "I haven't seen him this morning."

"He's holding his own." At the very least, their father was putting up a good front. "I'm trying to keep him busy—and productive," she emphasized. "The less time he has to think about Uncle Dan's death right now, the better."

"He's going to have to think about it sometime," Cris pointed out.

"Yes, I know. Time might not heal all wounds, but it'll help him cope."

Cris paused to smile at her. "You surprise me sometimes, Alex," she confessed. "You're like a rock, you know?"

"All hard and hilly?"

The question hadn't come from Alex. It came from Wyatt as he walked into the kitchen in time to catch the tail end of their conversation.

"I'm sure she meant solid," Alex informed him coolly. "What are you doing here?"

"You're having funeral services for my father tomorrow, remember?" She couldn't tell if he was being serious or pulling her leg. His expression was completely unreadable. He would have probably made a decent C.I.A. agent, she judged.

"I didn't mean *here*," Alex said impatiently, gesturing vaguely around the area and indicating the inn in general. "But *here*." This time her gesture only took in the kitchen where they were standing and where he, as far as she was concerned, was invading. "Aren't you supposed to be out there, directing traffic and handing out maps?"

"My dad's friends are all fairly intelligent people. They're capable of ringing the bell on the desk if they need anything."

"Are you looking for me?" That was the only reason she could fathom for why he'd left the reception area.

"Hard as it might be to believe, no. I just spent a good part of the morning standing next to you, so no, I'm not looking for you.

I was hoping I could grab something to eat, if that's okay with you?" He directed his question to Cris.

Abandoning the huge mixing bowl, Cris quickly crossed to the refrigerator, wiping her hands on the apron she always wore in the kitchen.

"Of course," she told him cheerfully. "What can I get you?"

"Anything," Wyatt said. "Any of that stew you made last night still left?"

"Absolutely," Cris responded, reaching into the back of the fridge for the industrial pot with the leftovers in it. "Alex, you want some, too, while I'm at it?"

Alex started to demur, but then her stomach picked that moment to rumble a protest rather loudly. Alex realized that she hadn't had breakfast yet and here it was, past lunch. She might be less cranky if she had something besides coffee in her stomach.

"Just a couple of bites," she told Cris.

Cris quickly heated the pot of stew while they watched awkwardly, without speaking, then filled two bowls and placed them on the countertop.

"There you go. Why don't you eat that in the dining room?" she suggested, nodding toward the swinging door and the room beyond it.

Wyatt met her suggestion with a grin. "Are you trying to get rid of us?"

"It's just a nicer atmosphere in the dining room," Cris responded.

"I don't need atmosphere," Alex protested.

Cris pretended she didn't hear her. "Besides, you're underfoot. The kitchen is only so large."

"I think we're politely being thrown out," Wyatt observed, picking up not only his bowl, but Alex's, as well. He backed through the swinging door into the dining room. Holding it open with his shoulder, he glanced at Alex. "Coming?"

"Well, as long as you're holding my lunch hostage, I guess I have to," she responded wryly.

There was only one other table occupied at the moment. Although breakfast was included in the price of an overnight stay at the inn, lunch and dinner were not. Though Cris made a menu available for lunch and dinner, most guests preferred going out to enjoy the various diversions that San Diego had to offer.

Wyatt sat after Alex took her seat. He began eating with relish. Neither one of them spoke for several minutes.

But the silence began to wear on his nerves and Wyatt finally broke it by saying, "Looks like everything's going smoothly."

Alex raised her eyes. "Were you expecting that it wouldn't?"

"That wasn't a challenge, Alex," he told her. "That was an attempt at a conversation."

"Oh. Okay," she returned. "Glad you cleared that up for me. Yes, everything's going smoothly so far."

He would have said, strictly based on their present exchange, that he and Alex were destined to never get along. Except that he knew better. There were times when they actually got along very well. So well that it started him thinking…until one or the other of them set off the competitive fireworks again.

"I appreciate all the trouble you're going to."

"I'm not doing it for you, I'm doing it for my dad. I want to make this as easy for him as possible. And I also want to give Uncle Dan the send-off he deserves." She paused. "Were you really serious about sticking around after the funeral?"

He thought she'd understood. "I promised my father I would finish the book about the inn for him," he repeated.

"I get that," she stressed. "But do you physically actually have to *stay* here at the inn while you write it?"

"Why?" he asked, guessing at what was going through her mind. "Not looking forward to having me around for two months?"

"Two months?" Alex echoed as if she'd just been told her prison sentence had doubled.

Again, his expression was unreadable. She could only hope he was kidding. "Maybe longer. It takes time to write a book."

Two months—or more—of tripping over Wyatt. Of seeing him every day. Of trying not to react to him half a dozen times a day.... This was going to be worse than putting up with him one month in the summer. "But wouldn't it be easier doing it in familiar surroundings?"

"Ladera is like a second home to me, so it *is* a familiar surrounding," he pointed out. "I know my way around here a lot better than I know my way around my place. I just bought the house six months ago."

"More like nine," she absently corrected him.

He stopped eating and looked at her in surprise. "How would you know that?"

Alex bit her lower lip. She'd realized the mistake she'd made just as he had picked up on it. She tried to act nonchalant as she shrugged. "I saw a blurb about it in one of the Sunday real estate sections a while back. Seems that they were temporarily experiencing a shortage of *real* celebrities buying or selling their homes to write about so they had to lower their standards and use anyone they could come up with.

That was the edition that had your house in it."

"All you had to say was that my dad told you about my new house when he was here a few weeks ago," he said, laughing. "So you've been reading about me?"

Alex bristled at his amusement, realizing that she wasn't fooling him at all. "It's not like I went looking for information about you, it was just there, staring me in the face. So I read it."

His grin was wide.

"I see."

No, he didn't, Alex thought, struggling to bank her annoyance. Wyatt was being smug—and it was her own fault. She'd walked right into it. When was she ever going to learn to think before she spoke?

It was a shortcoming she was going to have to work on. Starting *now*.

CHAPTER EIGHT

As SHE LEFT the dining room and began to head back to the reception area, Alex could hear someone ringing the bell on the front desk.

Repeatedly.

Had she not just left him behind at the dining room table, her first reaction would have been to think that Wyatt was trying to get her to hustle back. But, unless he'd learned how to move faster than the speed of light, it couldn't have been Wyatt.

Alex quickened her pace. Just what was so terribly important that it had prompted such a display of impatience?

She was going to be glad when this funeral was finally behind her.

For more reasons than one.

Alex really didn't like funerals, didn't like the pain and the grief associated with them. The services, no matter how beautiful or heartfelt, were always hard on everyone.

Approaching the reception desk, Alex slowed her pace. "Stacy?" she asked uncertainly. Even as she said the woman's name, she silently upbraided herself. How could she have forgotten about Stacy arriving today?

The brunette on the other side of the desk turned at the sound of her name. As attractive and perfectly made-up as ever, her college friend broke into a huge smile.

"Alex!" she cried, hurrying to the other side of the desk, tottering ever so slightly in what looked like five-inch heels. "It's really you! It's been so long, I was beginning to think I made you up."

"Not possible. Nobody has that kind of an imagination," Wyatt said dryly, walking in behind them.

Stacy Thompson stopped midhug. As she took in the man behind them, Alex could tell that her friend's female radar was instantly activated.

"And who's this?" she asked Alex, very openly and appreciatively staring at Wyatt.

Good old Stacy, still true to her colors, Alex thought, and very much on the prowl. Stacy had always had an eye for good-looking men and, no matter what else Wyatt might be, she had to concede he really was a good-looking man.

"Wyatt Taylor," Alex said. Then, to forestall Stacy from making any moves, she added, "We're holding funeral services for his father here tomorrow. His father was my dad's best friend." With that out of the way, she proceeded to make introductions. "Wyatt, this is Stacy Thompson. Stacy, Wyatt."

"Hi," Wyatt said simply, sticking out his hand. Because of where he lived and worked, Wyatt could easily recognize a barracuda when he saw one.

Stacy instantly took his hand in both of hers. Her eyes never left his. "I'm so sorry for your loss. I never had the good fortune to meet your father, but I'm sure he was a fine person."

There was nothing he disliked more than

empty words, even though he knew that at a time like this, he would be hearing a lot of them from well-intentioned people.

Still, he could resist answering the shapely brunette with a question. "What makes you say that?"

She hesitated and looked first at Alex before explaining. "Well, if he wasn't, there wouldn't be so many cars in the parking lot." She glanced at Alex a second time, and then a thought seemed to occur to her. "You didn't give away my room, did you? Please tell me it's still waiting for me." Her friend's sharp brown eyes gave Wyatt another once-over and her smile widened. "Although, I guess I could always bunk in with someone." She turned on the full force of her smile. "Did you know that before the turn of the twentieth century, travelers used to share their hotel room—and their bed—with total strangers while journeying out west? It was because there were so few places for them to stay."

"Still studying history, I see," Alex replied. History and marketing were the two subjects Stacy had studied when they'd been at the University of San Diego. But her real major had been men. Alex had always admired the other woman's frank honesty in her appreciation of the opposite sex. "Your room is still empty and waiting for you," she said with a knowing smile.

Stacy looked pointedly at Wyatt. "Maybe some other time, then," she murmured. She turned back to Alex. "Can you really put all these people up? I know you told me that your dad was expanding the inn, but it doesn't look all that much bigger since the last time I saw it."

"We've added four more rooms since then." And the plans for the next four were now officially on hold until she found someone to replace J. D. Clarke, the general contractor she'd fired yesterday.

"Just four?" Stacy frowned. "Then how are you going to accommodate all these people?"

"We're not," Alex replied simply. "Most of them are just stopping here to find out about the service. I'm referring them to the Fairmont."

Stacy laughed as she shook her head. "You always were a Girl Scout."

It was Alex's turn to laugh. "As I remember, that's Stacy-speak for boring pushover."

Stacy winced ever so slightly. "You really do have too good a memory. Like an elephant," she said in an aside to Wyatt. "She remembers every flaw, every embarrassing moment."

The last thing she wanted was for Stacy to begin rattling off episodes from their college years in front of Wyatt.

"We can catch up later," Alex told her quickly. She came around the desk arm in arm with the other woman to where she'd dropped her suitcase. "Why don't I take you to your room and you can settle in?" she suggested brightly.

"That's okay, I've got it," Wyatt told her, picking up Stacy's suitcase before she had a chance to. Behind them, the front door opened and then closed as several more people came in. "Which room?" he asked.

She would have rather she'd taken Stacy to her room while he dealt with the new guests, but she didn't protest. She didn't want to shirk her duties or even—knowing how Wyatt's mind worked—appear to be, of all things, territorial when it came to him. So she relinquished her friend's arm, handing Stacy over to Wyatt.

"I have Stacy in the Queen Victoria Room," she told Wyatt. It's a very good thing she hadn't accidentally doublebooked the room when she'd forgotten Stacy was coming. "That's the third one on—"

"I know where it is." Wyatt gave Stacy an easy smile. "After spending close to twenty summers here, I do know the layout."

"You lived here?" Stacy asked, clearly ready to hang on his every word.

"No, I visited here," he corrected her. "Every summer. With my dad."

She hooked her arm through his. Without breaking eye contact, her attention riveted to him, they walked out of the reception area.

"Oh," Alex heard her friend exclaim sympathetically. "Then his passing must be even more painful for you, since this is the beginning of summer and all…."

Alex didn't hear his answer. They had moved out of earshot.

Just as well, she told herself. The only problem was, she wasn't buying what she was selling.

"Miss," the tall, heavyset man on the other side of the desk said.

"Yes, I'm sorry," she apologized, pulling herself together. "What can I do for you, sir?" She smiled first at the man and then at the woman he was with.

He looked down at the crumpled paper he'd pulled out of his pocket, then back at her again. "I'm not sure we're in the right place, but we're in town for the funeral of an old friend tomorrow—"

"Oh, you're in the right place," Alex assured them, doing her best to put the couple at ease. She pulled over the list of names Wyatt had given her. She'd rewritten them in alphabetical order. "If you could just give me your names…?"

"Jacob and Marjorie Trudeau."

She could just faintly detect the sound of Stacy's laughter.

Some things never changed, she thought as she went down the list, searching for Trudeau.

Right after graduation, the ink barely dry on her diploma, Stacy had gotten a job with a high-powered national marketing firm in San Francisco.

She'd been envious of Stacy back then. Her friend was going to get to travel first-class all over the country for the firm, seeing exciting places while she worked with clients.

When Stacy eventually landed her own international account, the postcards began arriving from more exotic locations. Places Alex knew she was never going to be able to visit because she had become all but indispensable to her father at the inn.

"And you say this is a good hotel?" Jacob Trudeau was asking her, holding the sheet she'd given him with directions and the next day's itinerary.

"Absolutely, sir."

"Why can't we stay here?" Marjorie

Trudeau asked. She looked around the reception area and it was obvious she liked what she saw. "It looks so very charming and cozy. Doesn't it, Jake?"

"Uh-huh." Her husband responded like a man who knew better than to disagree with his wife in public.

Alex smiled at the compliment. "Thank you. We do our best, but I'm afraid we are completely booked right now. This… event…was rather an unexpected turn of events," she explained.

Trudeau, a retired journalist, his wife had proudly related while Alex was supplying directions to the Fairmont, appeared to be in no hurry to leave the inn.

"Dan used to talk about this place," he told Alex. "Said how much he looked forward to coming here every summer. Sometimes, he said, coming here was the only thing that kept him going," Trudeau added. "He said that the man who owned the inn and his daughters were like his own family. Aside from his son, he didn't really have any—but you probably already know that."

"Yes, I do," Alex replied, doing her best

to smile. She could feel herself tearing up. She expected she would do that, off and on, until Uncle Dan's death was something she became accustomed to. Something that didn't suddenly jump out at her.

She'd gone through the same painful journey when her mother had died, so she knew exactly what she was up against.

Though they were all mourning the loss of an exceptionally kind, decent human being, to Alex grief was private, something she might grudgingly share with family— on occasion—but not others.

"We were all very fond of him, too," she replied. "For years, I actually thought he *was* my uncle. I had been calling him Uncle Dan since before I can remember."

She could see Uncle Dan's friend was trying to place her. "You're…"

"Alex," she supplied.

He nodded, sharing a look with his wife. "The energetic one who always kept everything running," he concluded.

"Is that how he described me?" Alex asked, unable to tamp down her curiosity. In a way, talking about Dan this way was like still having him around—at least for a little while longer.

"Oh, that and a lot more." Trudeau folded the page of directions in two and tucked it in his pocket. "Well, Alex, it was nice meeting you after all this time. Marjorie and I will be back tomorrow for the service."

"And don't forget the reception," Alex added. "It'll be held outside near the ocean right after the service." She smiled warmly at the couple. "We have no intentions of sending you away hungry. Uncle Dan would have never forgiven us."

Trudeau laughed. "Sounds good." His arm around his wife's shoulders, he began to usher her toward the front door.

"Honey, maybe we can book a room for later this year," his wife suggested.

"That sounds like a good idea to me," her husband agreed wholeheartedly. He glanced back at Alex, one eyebrow raised.

"Come see me after the service," she told the couple. "If you give me an approximate date, I'll see what I can arrange for you."

Alex smiled to herself. Uncle Dan was

gone and the man was still doing them good. Sending business their way at his funeral.

She waited a few more minutes behind the desk. When no one else came in, she decided to go check on Stacy.

As she turned to walk toward the right wing of the inn, where the Queen Victoria Room—and Stacy—were, she saw Wyatt returning. He had a very bemused expression on his face.

"Is Stacy settled in yet?" she asked.

"No," he answered. "Not yet. I left her unpacking."

That struck her as odd. Stacy didn't unpack. She traveled so much, she'd once confided that she just left her suitcase open on the luggage stand and kept it zipped against the possibility of bedbugs, only taking out what she needed as she needed it.

"Your friend always hit on people she doesn't know?" Wyatt asked out of the blue.

Alex stared at him, trying to gauge whether Wyatt was amused or annoyed. She really couldn't tell. Wyatt had that poker face on again, and she'd never been able to crack it.

"She doesn't see it that way," Alex told him.

Her answer didn't make any sense to him. "What way?"

"That she doesn't know you. You asked if she always hits on strangers," she reminded him. "She doesn't think of you as a stranger."

If anything, that made even *less* sense. "Why would she know me?" And then an answer suggested itself. "Unless, of course," he said slowly, even though he knew the odds of what he was about to propose being true were pretty slim, "you talk about me."

She snorted. "Sorry to shoot you down," she told him, "but it's not what you think."

"Oh?" he asked innocently, growing more convinced that maybe Alex *did* talk about him to her friends. Did that mean that she thought about him once in a while? Or did talking about him only involve complaining?

"Stacy always says the only difference

between a stranger and a friend is an introduction—and I took care of that part when I told you her name and gave her yours. In Stacy's world, that makes you two old friends and hitting on an old friend is allowed."

Before she could stop herself, her curiosity got the better of her and she asked, "Was she successful?"

When he looked at her quizzically, Alex wasn't fooled. He knew *exactly* what she was asking, but for the sake of brevity, she spelled it out. "In hitting on you. Was she successful hitting on you?"

"No. I pretended not to know what she was getting at."

Was that because he was honorable or because he was still hurting too much to think along those lines right now?

"I apologize for her behavior," Alex said earnestly. "This is a bad time for you—although," she reconsidered, "maybe you could do with the distraction."

For a moment his eyes held hers and she realized that she'd stopped breathing for that tiny space of time. She chastised herself. Something was definitely off in her world.

"When I want to be distracted, I'll let you know," Wyatt said. "And I think I can pick my own distraction."

Alex couldn't shake the feeling that he was putting her on notice.

CHAPTER NINE

IT FELT, ALEX THOUGHT, much later that evening as she slid bonelessly into one of the wicker chairs on the veranda, as if every single second of her day had been stuffed to the breaking point with details. Details she couldn't bring herself to delegate.

She didn't want to burden her father with them and she felt that Stevi wasn't quite experienced enough. It would have been like throwing her sister into the deep end of the pool before she'd taught her all the fundamentals of swimming.

What she did have Stevi doing was keeping Stacy company. Fortunately, her good friend understood the position Alex was in, and the last she'd seen of the pair, they were going shopping.

As for Andy, she was making sure Ricky

was taken care of so that Cris was free to devote herself to the food preparations.

She'd touched base with Reverend Edwards to make sure that nothing had suddenly come up between yesterday and today that might keep him from officiating at the funeral tomorrow. And to make sure he had the correct time.

She wasn't about to leave a single thing to chance. Another reason why she had no social life, she thought, out of the blue. She had no idea how to let her hair down.

She'd made sure to accompany her father to the funeral home when he went to pay his last respects to the man he'd known since they'd first ridden their tricycles together growing up on Balboa Island.

She knew that her sisters had each made the pilgrimage from the inn to the funeral home and any one of them would have been willing to go with their father, but Alex felt that it was her responsibility to be there for him. That was her role, and she made sure she was there for him, to offer her moral support if he should need it.

Stacy, bless her, took it all in stride.

She'd initially informed her that she was very capable of entertaining herself, that she got around on her own in a great many cities across the country and didn't need anyone to hold her hand. When Stevi told her that she had no intentions of holding her hand unless she tripped on the sidewalk, Stacy had grinned and announced that they would get along just fine.

Alex had every confidence that they would. She was even a little envious of Stevi.

She was thinking about that just now when Stacy surprised her by sinking down into the wicker chair next to hers.

"So, how's it going with all the planning?" Stacy asked cheerfully.

Alex had always been honest to a fault but she saw no point in saying she was bone tired. Complaining never remedied anything. It certainly wouldn't help rejuvenate her, not tonight.

So she offered a vague, "I'm holding my own," and left it at that. Turning toward her, Alex said, "But I feel badly about not having any time for you today—or tomorrow."

Stacy waved her hand at the apology. "Hey, it's not as if your dad's friend died just to inconvenience me. I understand. We'll catch up after the reception is over with. I've got five days."

"Only five?" That didn't jibe with what they'd talked about earlier in the year, when Stacy'd told her she was planning to come out to see her. "I thought you had two weeks you absolutely had to take or you were going to lose them."

"Seems there's a clause in my contract that says I can trade them in for pay if I've been with the company for five years— and I have."

"But you said that you really needed those two weeks to recharge," Alex reminded her.

Stacy nodded. "I know, I know." She hesitated for a second, then plowed right in to give her the real reason for the abbreviated vacation. "But, Alex, if I step off that merry-go-round, even for a week, all these vultures are circling, just waiting to pounce, to take my place the second I'm not there. To do what I do—and maybe better. I can't take a chance on that happening. I've worked too hard to let some eager go-getter usurp my job."

"But you have an incredibly solid work record," Alex said. "You haven't taken any time off since forever. Doesn't that count?"

"They have very short memories," Stacy said with a sigh. "You're only as good as your next project."

Alex looked at her. Until this moment she hadn't realized just how good her life was in comparison to Stacy's. Any envy she had harbored vanished for good.

For a second Alex debated not asking her next question. But they were friends and she cared about the woman. "Doesn't it ever get to you?" she asked Stacy.

"What do you mean?"

"That your life isn't your own? That they can send you off to any place they want at what amounts to a moment's notice, without any regard for any plans *you* might have?"

Against the backdrop of crickets chirping, Stacy took in a deep breath and shrugged.

"Yes, maybe a little, but then everyone's got something they don't like about their job, right?" She smiled uncomfortably. "You're thinking about that emergency trip I had to make to that New England plant on Christmas Eve, aren't you?"

Stacy had told her all about it—after the fact. "You had plans," Alex reminded her.

Rather than agree, Stacy became defensive. "I've also got a long-range goal and that trumps spending Christmas with my family. It's not like I've never spent it with them before—or won't again."

It was easy to take life for granted, Alex thought. But faced with Uncle Dan's funeral the next day, that was something she promised herself she was never going to do again. Moreover, Alex felt compelled to point out the obvious to her friend.

"That's probably what Wyatt thought about spending the summer here with his father. And now he won't get the chance anymore. The only thing definite about the future, Stace," she said, "is that there's nothing definite."

Stacy shifted in her chair and stared off into the darkness.

"Maybe," she finally said. "But I'd rather think that the future is whatever I make it. And I intend to make it absolutely fabulous." She emphasized the last word with feeling and then turned to look at Alex. "By the way, what's the story on Wyatt?"

"What do you mean?" Why she suddenly felt protective of Wyatt didn't quite make sense to her. But she did. "His father just died."

"Yes, I got that." There was a smattering of impatience in Stacy's voice. "But is he married, engaged, living with someone, something like that?" she asked. And then a thought hit her before Alex was able to answer. "You and he aren't involved, are you?" she asked. "Because if you are, I'm sorry. You know I wouldn't poach."

Completely caught off guard by the question, Alex could only stare at her friend, stunned. "Wyatt and me? Oh, no, no," she denied vigorously. "There's nothing going

on between the two of us and the only understanding he and I have is that we stay
out of each other's way as much as possible
whenever he's here. Most of the time when
we were growing up, one of us would be
looking for a way to torment the other."

Stacy didn't seem convinced by her protest. "From the way it looked to me, you've
obviously outgrown that phase."

"His father just died, Stacy," Alex
pointed out again, this time more firmly.
"This isn't exactly the time for me to slap
a Please Kick Me sign on his back."

Stacy was smiling to herself. "If you ask
me, this is the time to be very, very sym-
pathetic to the man. Offer him a shoulder
to cry on." Her smile widened.

Her protectiveness raised its head again.
"Stacy, he's off-limits."

"Then you *do* have something going on."
This time, Stacy made it sound more like
an accusation.

"No," Alex emphasized with feeling,
"but the man is grieving. I wouldn't exactly call him vulnerable, but maybe he is
under that thick layer of barbed wire he's

wrapped up in. I don't want you messing with his feelings, Stacy. Not at a time like this. Wait until he can hold his own with you."

"Now you're coming off like his big sister," her friend observed, tilting her head to study Alex.

"No, not a big sister," Alex denied. "For one thing, he's older. But maybe like a friend."

Alex tossed the idea around for a moment. Friendship. It wasn't entirely distasteful. Maybe she was mellowing—or just growing soft in the head.

"Maybe, after all this time, that's what I've become," she said. "At least, that's what I am at this moment. He needs to get through this with as little outside interference as possible."

Alex tried to appeal to her friend's kinder side. "Wyatt's already lost his mother. She died last year. His father was the only family he had left. This is a hard transition for him. With his father's death, he's officially nobody's kid. I mean, he hasn't said as much—and fortunately I'm not in a position to understand how hard that must be—but it's surely a difficult reality to accept." Stacy, unlike her—and Wyatt—wasn't close to her family, and never had been. "All I'm doing is just backing off and letting him cope and find his way."

"Well, look at you, all philosophical and everything. You always were a poet," Stacy recalled.

"No poet," Alex contradicted, uncomfortable with the description. "I just put myself in his shoes."

"Well, I can see how he must feel very alone right now," Stacy said thoughtfully. She seemed almost intrigued by the notion.

"Stacy…" Alex warned.

"Did I say anything? I'm merely sympathizing with his lonely situation. Anyway—" she yawned "—I think I'm going to turn in. See you in the morning, Alex. Try to get some sleep. You don't want to look like hell tomorrow."

Alex wondered if that was Stacy's subtle way of saying she looked like hell now.

"See you tomorrow," Alex echoed as

her friend squeezed her shoulder and went inside.

Alex closed her eyes. She'd come out here to grab just one peaceful moment for herself.

That's what bedrooms are for, she upbraided herself.

Spreading her hands on the white wicker armrests, she was about to push herself to her feet when she heard a deep male voice say, "I never thought I'd see the day—or night—when you ran interference for me."

Her eyes flew open instantly and she found herself staring up at Wyatt, who was standing over her. Where had he come from?

"How did you overhear?" she demanded.

He pointed to the side of the house. "The neat thing about a wraparound veranda is that if you pick just the right place to sit, no one can see you."

"So you were spying," Alex concluded. That was *so* like him, she thought, annoyed.

"No," Wyatt contradicted. "I was sitting. Alone, I might add, until you claimed a chair by the door and your little friend found you."

She wasn't finished being annoyed with him. "I thought you outgrew eavesdropping."

He laughed. "I'm a writer, remember? I eavesdrop for a living. It's how I'm able to imitate people's cadences, make the things they say sound natural. I'm always searching for decent inspiration. Listening supplies me with input."

"You were eavesdropping," she countered.

"A rose by any other name…"

"Would still be eavesdropping," Alex snapped. She tried to remember if she'd said anything the least bit revealing or embarrassing, something he could hold over her head to amuse himself after his father's funeral was part of their history. "You could have cleared your throat, made some kind of a noise to let me know you were there."

"And miss the opportunity to hear you make Miss Too-Sexy-For-Words back off?" he asked in amusement. "Never."

It took effort to keep her mouth from dropping open. "You think Stacy's too sexy for words?" Alex asked, not completely comprehending why that would bother her at all, not to mention as much as it did.

"No," he answered mildly, "but she does. You can see it in her body language, the way she carries herself, tilts her head. Not that, in my shallow youth, I wouldn't have been attracted."

"But now that you're an old man, you wouldn't?" Alex asked, the question only partly tongue-in-cheek.

"Not an old man," Wyatt corrected her, "just not an easily swayed adolescent anymore."

"So you're telling me that you're more discerning now." She wasn't sure she believed him. After all, there were those photos of him with that model at one of the premieres—and there had been other, equally vapid-looking women, according to random stories on the internet.

"I'd like to think so. These days," he told her, "I'm more interested in substance than flash and fire."

"Substance," Alex repeated, sarcastically.

Wyatt pretended not to notice. "That's what I just said."

Her eyes never left his. She was waiting for him to blink. "You."

"Me," he verified. "Are we having a communication problem here?" he asked genially. "Because I can attest to the fact that you and I are the only ones sitting out here, so it shouldn't be so hard to grasp the concept that I'm talking about me."

"We're not having a communication problem," she said. "What we're having is a reality disconnect. The last picture I saw of you was at the Hollywood premiere of your latest movie—the title escapes me now, but it was a mere four months ago." There'd been a nubile blonde clinging to his arm for all she was worth. "The woman photographed with you not only appeared to be short on substance, but she was short on material, too. As in the material that went into making her dress—or, in this case, her almost nonexistent dress. Women of substance, to borrow your term, don't really go in for playing show-and-tell with their body parts."

Wyatt looked completely unfazed by her accusation. "Ava was my producer's daughter. She'd never been to a premiere before. I took her to mine as a favor to him."

Right, like she believed that. The man was a writer, obviously able to come up with an excuse at the drop of a hat. "Always the selfless giver, that's you."

"After the premiere," he continued as if he hadn't been interrupted, "I took her home to her father."

"How long after?" Alex really didn't expect an answer. She expected him to shut her down and walk back inside, annoyed.

"Immediately after," he answered, surprising her. "That was the arrangement I made with him—and with her. Ava was definitely too young to party, no matter how much she wanted to," he emphasized.

"And she didn't breathe a little heavily up close against you?" she asked, refusing to admit she'd been wrong.

"Oh, maybe just a little," Wyatt conceded.

"Aha."

"No, 'aha,'" he informed her firmly. "Ava tried to use her still-underdeveloped feminine wiles on me—and I said no. Besides, I'd given my word to her father that she would be home right after the movie and since he'd helped edit the film, I knew *he* knew *exactly* how long the movie ran and how long it would take to get home from the premiere at that time of night. Her father had left nothing to chance."

A man after my own heart, Alex couldn't help thinking. "That must have really put a crimp in your style."

"It would have," he agreed, "if I was into girls barely out of their teens—which I'm not. Even when I was in my teens, I wasn't into girls the same age as I was." There was a somewhat nostalgic smile on his lips.

Alex rolled her eyes. How had they gotten to this point? She didn't want an overview of his former—or present—love life.

"I can only imagine why."

"Well, let me take the mystery out of it for you," Wyatt offered. "Older women are more interesting conversationalists."

Okay, now he was *really* pulling her leg. "Conversationalists," she echoed.

"Yes."

The smile on his lips was positively wicked and completely unnerving. She decided it was time to end this exchange. She was too tired to win and she wasn't about to let him win by default.

"I suggest we both turn in," she said, rising to her feet.

His wicked smile spread. "Do you, now?"

She realized her error in her choice of wording. What was it about this man that made her feel as if she was forever losing ground? She could feel her cheeks heating.

"Separately," she elaborated. "Turn in to our *separate* rooms."

Wyatt spread his hands wide. The innocent smile was anything but. "I never thought you meant anything else."

The pending funeral curtailed her automatic reaction. Otherwise, she would have been exceedingly tempted to throw something fast and heavy at his head.

It made her long, just for a second, for the freedom of the past.

"Good night," she said, turning on her heel and marching inside.

"Good night," he echoed cheerfully, following in her wake.

CHAPTER TEN

THE MORNING OF the funeral, Alex was up before first light.

She hit the ground running.

The first thing she did, even before brushing her teeth, was to make another list.

Even so, she had an uneasy feeling that she'd forgotten something.

The decision to hold the service outdoors, down on a spit of land overlooking the Pacific Ocean, had required the temporary acquisition of an army of folding chairs, not to mention a level platform for the minister as well as the casket, the flowers and the enlarged photograph of Uncle Dan, showing him with his arm over the shoulder of a young Iraqi boy. He'd been at the height of his career and the prime of his life. He looked far too vital in the photograph to be felled by anything that life could possibly throw at him.

It was Wyatt's favorite photograph of Dan.

In her bright turquoise dress she wanted to join Wyatt in celebrating his father's life rather than his death—something he'd made clear he'd wanted "when my time comes." Surveying the immediate area, she felt satisfied that at least here, everything was proceeding according to schedule—more or less.

People had begun arriving and after the initial two or three had hesitantly approached the area chosen for the solemn occasion, Alex felt comfortable about leaving the mourners to take care of one another. Especially after Stevi and her father joined them.

A quick pass through the kitchen told her that Cris and Rosemary had everything under control. Food for the reception would be ready on time.

As she left, Alex nodded at Andy, silently thanking her for keeping their nephew occupied and out of Cris's hair.

Checking her phone she saw she had two text messages. One was from the minister—whose message contained misspellings, testifying to how unaccustomed he was to this mode of communication—and the other was to let her know that the casket was en route from the funeral home ahead of schedule.

Alex was about to go back outside again when something made her stop.

And then she remembered what she'd forgotten to put on her long list.

Wyatt.

Alex backtracked through the inn and stopped in front of the room her father had told Wyatt he could claim as his own for as long as he liked. The door was closed. Alex stood in front of it, debating her next move.

Common sense told her to just turn around and go back to the ocean to await the minister's arrival. A gut feeling, however, told her to stay where she was and knock.

Alex wanted to make sure Wyatt wasn't in his room the way an uneasy feeling whispered that he might be. She had no idea what to call that uneasy feeling.

Since it definitely wasn't that she was in tune to the man.

You know he's not going to welcome you butting in if he is inside the room. Alex raised her hand anyway and knocked on the door. Softly.

There was no response from inside.

There, satisfied? He's not there. Now go!

But she didn't. She remained where she was and after a moment more, chewing thoughtfully on her lower lip, Alex knocked again, louder this time. When there was still no response, she knocked a third time, louder still.

Then, completely against every instinct, she tried the doorknob. It gave under her hand, allowing her to open the door.

She did.

Slowly.

Of course, Alex reasoned, Wyatt actually might *not* be in the room. He might be somewhere on the grounds and she'd just missed him. But somehow, something deep in her gut told her that Wyatt wasn't on the grounds, he was here, in his room, and he needed to have someone come and get him moving.

That was her job.

Finally she opened the door wide enough to be able to look inside.

Wyatt was there, in the room, standing to the far left of the door. His back was to her and, hands shoved deep into his pockets, he was looking out the window. Tension fairly radiated from him.

"Didn't you hear me knock?" Alex asked softly, like someone speaking on the phone in a nursery filled with sleeping infants.

"I heard you," Wyatt replied gruffly, still not turning to face her. "I was just hoping you would go away."

He'd been dressed and ready to attend the funeral for more than half an hour now, but he couldn't get himself to walk out the door, because, until he did, until he witnessed the ceremony and watched the casket being lowered into the ground, he could go on pretending that this wasn't real. That his father was still out there somewhere, doing what he'd always done.

He'd had no idea how much he didn't want to let go of his father, of the past, until this morning.

He hurt so badly, he thought his heart was going to split in two.

"Why?" she asked quietly, crossing to Wyatt in deliberate, measured steps.

"Do I have to have a reason?" he snapped, impatient and weary at the same time.

"Wyatt—" she placed her hand gently on his rigid shoulder "—you can't hide in here."

He swung around then, denial hot on his lips. A denial he didn't voice because when he looked at her, the uselessness of the effort hit him right between the eyes.

"Why is it you've always had this knack of getting into my head and using what you find there against me?" he asked. "Ever since we were kids."

The corners of her mouth curved ever so slightly. He guessed she was remembering an incident or two.

"I'm not clairvoyant, I was just good at making you feel paranoid."

He took a deep breath, willing his tension to leave him. He managed to succeed, but only in part. He was a grown man. He had thought it was going to be easier than this. But it wasn't, and being a grown man had nothing to do with it.

"Once I go outside, it's all over. There'll never be another summer with my father. There'll never be another deep-sea fishing trip, or long evenings on the veranda, talking, wondering why all the fireflies were back east—"

"Maybe they don't get along with the june bugs," she suggested, a sad smile playing along her lips. It was an argument she'd put forth when she and his father had had the same discussion years ago. Uncle Dan had laughed then. She'd loved making him laugh. It was why she remembered the exchange.

"Yeah, maybe." Wyatt laughed softly now himself. He looked into her eyes. "I don't know if I can handle it, Alex."

Though she sympathized with what he was saying, she knew she couldn't let him stay here. It would only be worse for him down the line.

"Wyatt, he's gone whether you accept it or not, whether you attend the service or not," she said quietly. "And if you don't attend the service, you'll regret it in time. *Really* regret it. You know that."

He closed his eyes and sighed wearily. "Yeah, I know that." Opening his eyes again, he added, "You're right—and if you ever tell anyone I said so, I'll deny it with my dying breath."

She laughed, nodding. "Your secret's safe with me. Now put that on—" she nodded at the jacket laid out on his bed "—and let's go. A lot of your father's friends are already here."

He picked up the jacket and slipped it on, but as he did, his collar ended half sticking up. Wyatt didn't notice.

Looking back at him, Alex did.

"Hold it," she said.

He looked at her quizzically, and she carefully smoothed his collar down. They stood there for a moment, looking at each other. Feeling things she wouldn't put a name to.

Alex dropped her hands to her sides.

"Okay, good to go," she pronounced, turning to walk out the door.

"Why did you come just now?" he asked, following Alex out. He lengthened his stride and caught up to her so that they went down the hall to the rear exit together.

She was about to shrug and say something about his being an item on her "to do" list and wanting to check him off, but that really wasn't the truth. She'd been concerned about him and, right now, he needed the truth.

"I didn't see you around so I just wanted to check on you, make sure everything was all right—and give you a little push out the door if you needed it," she concluded. "Something I'm very capable of."

"You *are* pushy," Wyatt acknowledged, but there was no edge in his voice, no combativeness. Only humor.

Alex tossed her head. "Lucky for you that I am," she retorted.

Expecting a flippant remark from him, his response caught her completely by surprise. "Yeah, I guess it was lucky for me."

Just as she was about to push open the

back door to go outside, Wyatt put his hand on her shoulder. Another round of cold feet? Alex was prepared to give him another pep talk if she had to.

But as she opened her mouth, Wyatt took the wind out of her sails by quietly saying, "Thanks."

She could only smile. After a beat, she murmured, "Don't mention it." But he was already outside and heading toward the large crowd of people who had been steadily arriving while he had been inside the inn, talking to her.

THE SERVICE WENT ON a great deal longer than Alex had anticipated.

When he was finished his short service that had come touchingly from the heart, the minister opened the floor to anyone else who wanted to say a few words.

It turned out there were more than a few people who did.

Alex's father had been the first to talk about his lifelong friendship with the journalist. After that, almost half the guests felt the need to share either their feelings, or,

MARIE FERRARELLA   191

more often, a story about the man whose
presence was going to not only be missed,
but acutely missed.

Even Alex, who never liked to speak in
front of an audience, felt compelled to say
several words of tribute about the man she
would always fondly think of as "Uncle
Dan."

She deliberately kept her remarks short,
afraid that if she didn't, she would break
down. The display, she felt, would be embarrassing and not exactly helpful for
Wyatt to witness.

Although her father had been her pri-
mary concern ever since she'd heard of
Uncle Dan's death, after having found
Wyatt holed up in his room, she found her
sense of protectiveness split. And during
the service, she could feel it shifting and
weighing in on Wyatt's side.

The way she saw it, her father had Stevi,
as well as Cris and Andy, to rally and help
him through this very difficult time.

But although Wyatt was standing in
the midst of a great many of his father's

friends, on a personal level, there was no wife, no significant other, to hold his hand.

There wasn't even a best friend here who could offer him a shoulder to lean on. For that matter, she didn't even know if Wyatt *had* anyone who fit that description. In her opinion, if Wyatt *had* had a best friend, that friend would have been here for him.

So, by process of elimination, that left her.

It wasn't that she saw herself as even a close friend, but they did go back a very long way. And besides, she hated seeing anyone in pain, physical or emotional, she told herself.

No other reason.

Tomorrow, when this was behind them and slowly becoming part of the tapestry of their past, things would go back to normal.

The minister looked out on the sea of faces as Alex walked away from the podium after concluding her tribute. "Is there anyone else here who would like to say something before we inter Daniel's earthly remains?"

Wyatt rose, walking up to the spot she

had just vacated. Watching him, Alex had to admit she was surprised. He'd told her he wasn't going to speak.

Obviously he'd had a change of heart.

Taking the podium, he looked out at the rows of filled chairs and appeared, to Alex, to be overwhelmed. She willed him to look in her direction and strived to make eye contact. When he did, she nodded and smiled.

Wyatt collected himself after a moment and said, "When I was a kid, I used to think that my dad had a strange job. A job that took him away to places with names I couldn't begin to pronounce for months at a time.

"It seemed like a lonely way to earn a living, separated from family and friends. More than anything, I wanted him to be like other dads who went to work and came home at the end of the day.

"But he wasn't like other dads. He was special. My father had the ability to make friends wherever he went—and he went everywhere. That was his real gift. That he could meet people and turn them into friends as easily as someone else saying,

'Good morning.' The reporting, the long investigations he conducted and then transmitted, they were just his sidelines. His *true* calling was to make friends. No one was immune to him."

He looked around at the gathering and smiled. "Today just goes to prove that I'm right. Didn't matter if they didn't see one another for years at a time, my dad kept friends for life."

Wyatt blew out a breath. He was struggling to keep his composure.

"And now he's off making new friends." Wyatt glanced up toward the cloudless sky. "But your friends down here are going to miss you, Dad. And none of them even begins to miss you as much as I do."

Wyatt pressed his lips together, trying to compose himself, then said, "See you soon." It was the last thing his father always said when he left for work.

Alex gave up wiping away her tears and just let them flow.

CHAPTER ELEVEN

LEAVING THE PODIUM, Wyatt returned to the first row and took his place between Alex and her father. As he passed Alex, he kept his eyes forward but wordlessly he took out his handkerchief and handed it to her.

Accepting it from him, Alex murmured, "Allergies."

Facing front now, Wyatt didn't spare her a glance. "Bad, this time of year."

Saying a few more words to the gathering, Reverend Edwards ended the service. People began filing out of the rows, their next stop the private cemetery where Dan Taylor's casket was to be interred.

Since it was a relatively short distance from the ocean to the cemetery, rather than transport the casket by the dark limousine that had initially brought it from the funeral home, Wyatt, her father and six other pallbearers from among Uncle Dan's friends carried it to the grave site.

The mourners, led by the minister, followed directly behind them.

Because there were so many mourners, it took a while for them to file by the casket one last time, leaving their long-stemmed red roses as a token of their sorrow.

Finally the casket was slowly lowered into the ground.

The solemnity of the act burned itself into Alex's heart. She felt her eyes stinging again.

After her father and Stevi had led the guests away to the reception, Wyatt remained standing over the gaping hole that was to be his father's final resting place. It was several seconds before he became aware that Alex was still there with him, standing on the other side of the grave.

Watching him.

"Don't worry," he assured her, "I'm not going to do anything stupid. You don't need to hover over me."

Alex lifted her shoulders in a careless shrug. "No place else I have to be."

He studied her, becoming slowly aware of his surroundings. And her. From what he'd seen, Alex's every moment was accounted for from when she got out of bed in the morning to when she fell back into it. His father used to marvel at how tirelessly she worked.

"Since when?"

"I make my own schedule," she said, moving around to his side of the grave.

He couldn't help smiling, just a little. "And exactly what is this listed under, 'hovering over bereft friend'?"

"No," Alex denied firmly in a slow, measured cadence. "For one thing, I wouldn't have cited you as being a friend. For another, I don't 'hover.' That description makes me sound like some deranged hummingbird searching for a place to land."

He laughed. "You don't fall into the hummingbird category." Before Alex could take offense at what might have sounded like a putdown to her, he pointed out, "Black Hawk helicopters hover."

"Better," she acknowledged loftily. "But for the record, I am *not* hovering. I'm just waiting to escort a guest of the inn to the reception."

A guest of the inn.

The formal title made him sound like a stranger.

"It's not like I don't know my way," he said dismissively. He was trying to make her back off. Trying to get a few more moments alone with his father one last time.

But Alex wouldn't leave.

She inclined her head. "Maybe today you don't." When he looked at her sharply, she went on to explain, "Today, your emotions are all over the place and you could be excused for not knowing that your fingers are at the end of your hand."

Frustration bit into him. "So you're hanging around to show me where my fingers are?"

The corners of her mouth curved slightly. "Something like that."

He felt himself growing unreasonably angry. "I don't need a babysitter."

"No one said you did," Alex countered genially.

He blew out a breath. The woman was

infuriatingly unmovable. "You're just going to keep standing there no matter what I say, until I'm ready to leave, aren't you?"

"Pretty much."

He sighed again, surrendering. "How is it no one's ever strangled you yet?"

She had an answer for that, too. "Well, for one thing, I know tai chi. I'm also a fast runner."

Squaring his shoulders, he moved back from the grave and gave every indication that he was ready to go. "That must be it."

She didn't want to rush him. "We can stay longer if you like."

But Wyatt shook his head as he started walking toward the inn and the reception that had been set up outside. "That's okay. Dad's not really here anymore, anyway."

Alex fell into place beside him.

About to say something about the service, it suddenly occurred to her that Wyatt was walking rather slowly. She doubted that the occasion had anything to do with it. He was doing it for her benefit.

"You don't have to walk slowly on my

account, Wyatt," she told him. "You can pick up the pace."

He looked down at her shoes. As usual, she was in heels. "You're wearing…what, three-inch heels?"

"Four," she corrected. "What does that have to do with anything?"

"We're on grass."

Alex curtailed the impulse to say that she could see what they were walking on and instead picked up her pace, passing him.

"Race you!" she declared with a laugh. The next second, she was moving across the grass as if it had suddenly turned to concrete.

He reacted without thinking.

With a laugh that echoed hers, Wyatt took her up on the challenge and picked up his own pace. Part of him was waiting for her to take a spill. The other part knew he was waiting in vain.

As they jogged toward the reception, he saw Andy, holding Ricky's hand, turn and watch their speedy approach. She looked concerned and then Ricky suddenly jerked free of her hold. The four-year-old pumped his little legs hard as he ran toward Wyatt, his arms opened wide.

"Wy!" he yelled.

Stooping down, Wyatt scooped the boy up in his arms and whirled him around twice. Ricky dissolved into giggles.

"Hi there, Ricky. How's my favorite guy?"

Now that he was no longer being whirled around, Ricky drew himself up in Wyatt's arms, as if that would make him seem taller, like a "big boy," which was what, according to the boy himself, he aspired to be more than anything else in the world.

"Oh-kay," he announced with enthusiasm. "How you?" he asked, doing his best to sound like the grown-ups who comprised most of his world.

"How *are* you," Alex corrected her nephew.

The boy looked at her, perplexed. "Oh-kay. How you?"

Wyatt laughed, the tension that had ridden roughshod over him all morning lessening. He hugged the small boy to him, affectionately ruffling his hair. "Give up," he told Alex.

Her eyes met Wyatt's and she looked at him for a long moment. And then she said in a very firm voice, "I never give up."

And, though he wouldn't have admitted it to her for the world because it would give Alex something to hold over his head, most likely until the end of time, today— for him—her not giving up had been a good thing.

Alex, he'd thought more than once—and said more than once in less-than-flattering terms when he'd been younger—was like a pit bull. She'd latch on to something with jaws of steel and she wouldn't let go until she got whatever it was that she was after.

She had him putting one foot in front of the other, making his way through this difficult day.

"What do you say we get ourselves something to eat?" Wyatt suggested to the boy in his arms. "I hear your mom's been working all morning, making some pretty terrific stuff."

"Yeah. Eat," Ricky cried excitedly. Twisting around in Wyatt's arms until he could see the long buffet tables that had been set up earlier this morning, the four-year-old pointed to them. "There!"

"I couldn't have said it better myself," Andy said. She reached for her nephew.

But Ricky shrank back, grasping the front of Wyatt's shirt.

"No," Ricky cried. "Wy!"

"It's okay," he told Andy with a reassuring smile. Ricky forced him to think about something other than his loss and the pain that went along with it. "I can hold on to him for a while. We're bonding, aren't we, Ricky?"

"Yes!" Ricky declared happily, despite the fact that Wyatt was fairly certain the boy had no idea what "bonding" meant.

Alex was secretly rather impressed with the way Wyatt was handling her nephew and really glad that he had this distraction to keep him busy.

"Good man," Wyatt said to the boy. And then he turned to Andy and suggested, "Why don't you and the Iron Maiden here—" he nodded in Alex's direction "—go get something to eat while you still can? The line looks like it's about to get huge any minute now."

Alex shook her head at the title he'd just bestowed on her. "Well, I can certainly see why they pay you the big bucks for those screenplays of yours. You obviously have such a *witty* way with words."

"Alex," Andy stressed reprovingly, tugging on her sister's sleeve as she indicated Wyatt with her eyes.

Alex pulled her arm free. "Excuse us," she said to Wyatt rather formally. With that, she pulled her sister aside.

Andy spoke up before she could. "Alex, how can you be so insensitive to Wyatt? This isn't just another day for him—"

Alex was surprised that Andy couldn't see what she was actually doing.

She hustled Andy over to the buffet line beneath the canopy she'd rented and picked up a couple of plates. "That's exactly the point, Andy. If I act all soft and sweet toward Wyatt, then it's *not* just another day. It's the day he buried his father, and letting him focus on nothing except that will be really terrible for him to put up with."

Déjà vu. She felt like she had to keep having this conversation with her family. If only they'd have a little more faith in her.

Setting the plates on the edge of the table in front of her, Alex slowly moved along the line, making choices and splitting them between the two plates.

"But if I bait him the way I always have, well, that's a little bit of normalcy he has to hang on to."

She spared Andy a glance and saw that her sister was filling her own plate.

Andy shrugged, clearly bemused. "I've never really understood what goes on between you and Wyatt."

"I do," Stevi interjected as she got in between her two sisters. She didn't have a plate with her, but was checking out the array of food Cris had set up. "Wyatt and our big sister seem to like to act like two adolescents—it's a feeble attempt on both their parts to deny that they're attracted to each other."

"For an artist, you're not very observant," Alex told her, picking up a couple of croissants and dividing them between the two plates. "As to your less-than-astute deduction—you're wrong. I wouldn't be attracted to him even if this was an island in the middle of the Pacific and Wyatt was the only other living male around besides Dad and Ricky."

"If he was, I'd fight you for him," Stevi assured Alex. Glancing over her shoulder in Wyatt's direction, her sister added, "I still might fight you for him just because."

Her curiosity aroused, Alex finally had to ask, "Because, what?"

Stevi stole another look and sighed soulfully. "Because he just keeps getting better looking every time I see him. He was already a ten-plus in my book."

Alex laughed dryly. "What you need, dear sister, is a new book."

Stevi's eyes narrowed. "Are you honestly going to stand there and tell me that you don't think he's good-looking?"

"I didn't say that I didn't think he was good-looking," Alex pointed out.

"Oh, so you *do* think he's good-looking." Stevi grinned as if she'd just won a victory.

Alex rolled her eyes as she deposited several crab cakes on one of the plates. "Stevi, looks have nothing to do with anything."

"His looks have *everything* to do with it," Stevi insisted.

Alex stared at Stevi for a long moment, caught off guard by her sister's reaction to someone who was like a brother to them all.

A thought suddenly occurred to her. She felt her stomach lurch.

"Have you and Wyatt…?" She let the question trail off and held her breath, waiting.

"Have he and I what, Alex?" Stevi asked, deadpan.

"Did you share…?" She still couldn't get herself to form the question, to define the wavering image that kept popping into her head.

"Did we share what?" Stevi asked innocently. "A joke? A sandwich? A kiss?"

"Yes, yes, and did you?"

Stevi apparently decided she'd had enough

fun and let her off the hook. "Nope. I think of him more in the big-brother light, and besides, if a kiss was going to happen, I figure that it would involve the two of you, not me."

Why was everyone so eager to see them as a couple? They weren't anything of the kind.

"How long have you suffered from this delusion?" Alex intoned, deliberately keeping her eyes on the two plates she was filling as she worked her way down the buffet table.

Stevi appeared to be thinking about her answer. "Pretty much ever since you and Wyatt were sophomores in high school."

"Long time to be wrong," Alex observed as she came to the end of the buffet. The two plates were fully loaded.

Stevi looked at the heaping platters in surprise. "Since when did you start eating that much?"

"Since I started making up a plate for Dad." She nodded over to where he stood chatting in the distance. "By the time he realizes he's hungry, there won't be anything left."

"And the second plate's yours?"

Alex didn't answer her. "Why don't you take this to Dad for me?" Not waiting for an answer, she all but shoved one of the plates into Stevi's hands.

With that, she turned on her heel and walked away.

"Hey, where're you going?" Stevi called after her.

"Somewhere else," was all Alex said as she kept on walking.

CHAPTER TWELVE

MAKING HER WAY across the grass, Alex found Wyatt still holding Ricky, perching the boy against his hip. He seemed so comfortable about it, it made her wonder if there might have been a girlfriend or two in his life who'd had a small child or children of her own.

Alex doubted he was acting on pure instinct alone. She knew for a fact he was an only child and as far as she'd gathered over the years, Wyatt had no uncles or aunts to afford him an extended family. That meant that there'd been no small children for him to babysit or play with.

Even so, Ricky had taken to him instantly. Granted, the boy was the living antithesis of shy, but the way he lit up around Wyatt was definitely a cut above even *his* normal behavior.

She took Ricky's reaction to Wyatt to be a testament to the latter's decent character.

Not that she would ever willingly tell him that.

"Trade you," she declared as she came up behind the pair.

When Wyatt turned and saw her, she took the boy from him with her free arm while, with her other hand, she handed Wyatt the plate she'd prepared for him.

Wyatt looked first at the teeming plate, then at her, clearly bemused and puzzled. "You're feeding me now?"

Alex took a better hold on Ricky, shifting him to her right side. She shrugged absently. Somehow, Wyatt had made it sound much too personal. "I loaded up the plate with food. What you do with it is up to you."

He popped a cherry tomato into his mouth. "Should I be listening for hoofbeats?"

Sometimes Alex thought that he was determined to talk over her head—and it never failed to annoy her when he did.

"Hoofbeats?"

Wyatt nodded. "With the approach of the Four Horseman of the Apocalypse."

"Horsies!" Ricky exclaimed gleefully, latching on to the only word that held any importance to him. "Where are horsies?"

"No, honey. There're no horsies, no hoofbeats." She looked at Wyatt pointedly. "And no apocalypse. I just don't want you keeling over from hunger near the inn. People will talk."

Wyatt was sampling the black bean salad and waited until he swallowed before commenting. "People might talk even more now if they see you actually being nice to me like this." He punctuated his statement by using his fork as an extension of his hand and pointing it at her.

Alex sniffed and tossed her head. "I'm always nice," she informed him, then looked to her nephew for backup. "Aren't I, Ricky?"

"Yes! You're nice," Ricky echoed, bobbing his head up and down. His silky, straight blond hair swayed back and forth as he did so.

Alex inclined her head, her triumph displayed as she nodded toward her nephew. "See, out of the mouths of babes."

Ricky took instant offense. "I'm not a baby," he protested.

"Of course you're not," she quickly agreed. "Out of the mouths of big boys. Better?" she asked, giving him a quick squeeze.

"Better," he responded with a wide smile, nodding again. When he turned his head toward Wyatt, he looked intently at the still overloaded plate his hero was holding in his hand.

There was no missing the interest in the boy's eyes.

"Hungry?" Wyatt asked.

"Hung-gree," Ricky confirmed.

Wyatt selected one of the mini croissants Alex had brought him. "How's this one?" he asked. "Looks like it's ham and cheese. You like ham and cheese, Ricky?"

Ricky stretched his arms out, wiggling his fingers.

But as Wyatt started to hand over the goods, Alex deliberately turned her body so that the croissant was suddenly out of her nephew's reach. Ricky made a high-pitched protest.

Alex looked at him very deliberately and asked, "Ricky, what do you say when someone offers you something and you want it?" They'd been through this several times before. She was just trying to hammer the lesson home.

Ricky appeared crestfallen, then looked at Wyatt and said in a very subdued voice, "Yes, peas."

The words, combined with the boy's deadly earnest expression, made Wyatt laugh. "Well, I don't see any peas on this plate, but here's a sandwich for you." He offered the mini croissant to the boy.

Releasing his hold on the back of her neck and trusting Alex to hold him steady, Ricky leaned over and grabbed the small croissant with both hands. The second he had it, he bit into it with gusto.

"Good!" Ricky declared, humming as he chewed.

"You be sure to tell your mama that," Alex said. "She's been preparing all this since before you woke up, little man."

"By herself?" Wyatt queried.

"No. Rosemary King came in at six this morning, bless her, and pitched right in."

"Rosemary King?" Wyatt repeated, a quizzical expression on his face. He was obviously trying to put a face to the name and for a moment, he was drawing a blank.

Alex nodded, keeping an eye on Ricky as he made short work of the croissant, eating it with such unrestrained enthusiasm, you'd have thought that it was the first meal he'd had in over twenty-four hours.

She loved seeing her nephew's innocent reaction to things. At four, he wasn't restricted by the dictates of the world around him. There were no pretenses. What you saw was what you got. If he liked something, you knew it, just as, if he didn't like something, he didn't hold that back, either.

"You've seen her at the inn before," she absently said to Wyatt. "Slender, in her late fifties, she's been to dinner a few times when you and your dad were here. Rosemary has a modest little house in the area. She's quiet, tends to blend into the background."

Wyatt laughed shortly. "Everyone does around you."

His comment caught her up short.

What are you up to? she wondered, looking at him.

On the surface, what he'd just said sounded like a compliment, but this was Wyatt and nothing was that simple if it involved him.

She pinned him with a long, probing look. "That's not a compliment, is it?"

He had to admit, he did enjoy confusing Alex. "That's an observation that you tend to drown everyone else out, not to mention make them fade into the background."

Still holding Ricky, she shifted him to her other side so she could get a clearer look at the enemy. "Are you saying I talk too much?" she challenged, her voice dangerously low.

Wyatt laughed. "Well, you certainly don't talk too little."

She studied him for a long moment, as if weighing whether or not to take offense, or to just roll with it.

After a moment's deliberation, Alex said, "Not bad, but you can do better."

"I'll work on it," he told her.

Alex nodded. "You do that." She kissed the boy in her arms. "Time to go find Andy and reunite you with your fun aunt."

"Why?" Ricky cried mournfully, twisting around so that he could see Wyatt more clearly. It was obvious that her nephew wanted to stay with him.

This time, Alex didn't shift to allow Ricky a better view.

"No, Wyatt's eating and then he has people to talk to. You can see him later." She'd already begun walking away, as she asked over her shoulder, "Are you *really* going to finish writing your dad's book on the history of the inn?"

He'd already rescheduled his other commitments. As far as he was concerned, this took priority over everything else. "I told you, I gave my father my word that I would finish it for him."

"And you'll be staying here until you're finished?" she asked.

Wyatt could sense her discomfort. He

smiled broadly. In days gone by, he knew that his grin alone would have been enough to set her off. But over the past couple of days, he'd become acutely aware of a different, far more complex Alex than he'd ever thought existed.

"Every single day until I finish it."

Alex groaned and rolled her eyes. "Just how far did your dad get with this book?"

"From the notes I saw, I'd say a little short of halfway through."

She moaned. She could feel desperation nibbling away at her. "And there's really a market for this?" she challenged.

Wyatt had always been practical in his own way. Working on something that wouldn't ultimately turn out to be profitable wasn't his style. Maybe he could be reasoned out of this—or at least made to postpone it.

"My dad's old publisher seems to think so."

"Does my father have final approval?" she asked.

Ricky had begun fidgeting and more than anything, she wanted to set the restless boy down, but she had a feeling he would take off like a shot and she didn't feel up to running after her nephew. He was faster than he had a right to be.

"Not that I'm aware of," Wyatt replied. Not wanting to raise his voice to be heard, he came closer. Ricky started leaning more and more in his direction. "My father never said anything to me about asking for your dad's final approval."

"But you could show it to my dad once you're finished with the first draft if you wanted to, right?"

Wyatt inclined his head. "*If* I wanted to."

She narrowed her eyes. She'd been that way all of her life: exceedingly protective of her family and most especially of her father. Not that she thought Wyatt would knowingly write something that might hurt either her family's reputation or her father, but then again, he could very well write something that might unexpectedly create negative repercussions for them.

"*Want* to," Alex instructed in a low, no-nonsense tone that a general might use when ordering recruits into battle.

"If you're trying to hypnotize me, it's not working. And threatening me with bodily harm stopped being effective the summer I finally grew taller than you," he reminded her.

She hadn't been contemplating bodily harm, but it did seem tempting. Granted she was by no means stronger than he was, but she was just as clever and the trick here would be to beat him to the punch, something that she'd managed to do a number of times in the past.

"How about threatening you with the fact that it's the right thing to do and you know it?"

Putting the verbal sparring temporarily on hold, Wyatt looked at her, seemingly mystified. "Why would you think I wouldn't do right by the inn—or your dad?"

"Because when you come right down to it, I don't trust you any further than I can throw you," she informed him. "Just remember, a book on the inn isn't a book about me, it's about my family. People who have always been nice to you."

The smile that played on Wyatt's lips was one she couldn't begin to fathom. All she knew was that it seemed to target the pit of her stomach, creating an odd, pinched feeling dead center that refused to go away.

"Except for you," he said, his gaze all but pinning her to the spot.

She raised her chin. "Like I said, this book isn't about me."

The fact that he didn't agree with her, but instead said nothing, made her uneasy. While she was confident Wyatt really *did* like her father and was fond of her sisters, she was also aware of the kind of relationship the two of them had had with each other over the years. There were times, she was willing to admit, when the one-upmanship got out of hand and though she wouldn't have said it out loud, it was usually her fault.

Would that affect the kind of book Wyatt wrote?

He was a decent enough person, but getting this sort of revenge had to be tempting.

She closed her eyes and blew out a breath. "This means I'm going to have to be nice to you until you finish writing this thing and get the galleys back from the publisher, doesn't it?"

"Well, I wouldn't want you to strain anything, now," he said.

Too late, she thought.

"Right," she muttered. "I'll see you later."

"Looking forward to it," he responded as she walked away.

Locating Andy, Alex entrusted Ricky and the care and feeding thereof to her youngest sister.

"Missed you, guy," Andy said, taking a firm hold of their nephew's hand and setting him on the ground. He tugged a couple of times, testing if he could get free, then surrendered to the inevitable—for now. "Was he with you all this time?" she asked Alex.

"Actually, most of the time he was with Wyatt." As she spoke, Alex scanned the crowd, looking to see if Wyatt had gone on to connect with any of his father's associates—and if so, who—purely out of innate curiosity, she told herself.

Stevi joined them for a moment, walking in on the last sentence. "There's a side of Wyatt I never thought I'd see," she told her sisters.

Alex wasn't sure just where she was going with this. "You mean, grieving?"

"No, I mean the way he was with our precious nephew here," she explained, bending to kiss the top of Ricky's head. The boy smiled up at her. "I was watching him earlier. Wyatt's really good with kids."

"Well, he's really good with Ricky, anyway," Alex qualified. What was it about the man that had her wanting to say "black" if the word "white" was associated with him?

Andy and Stevi exchanged confused looks. "And the difference being?" the latter asked.

"He likes Dad. He gets along with you two. I know he likes Cris. So he has to be nice to Ricky since he's Cris's son, Dad's grandson and your nephew."

"Not necessarily," Stevi countered stubbornly. "He could just ignore him. A lot of people don't know what to do around kids so they just ignore them, hoping the kids'll just go away."

Alex sighed. She had a pretty good idea what her sister was up to. "You don't have to try to build Wyatt up, Stevi, I'm being as nice to him as I possibly can, okay?"

Andy grinned, shaking her head. "And it hurts, doesn't it?"

"You have no idea." Alex pretended to clutch at the region where her heart was. "The pain is excruciating."

"Wait, let me go find a bullet for you to bite on," Stevi replied.

"Don't," Andy warned Stevi. "Knowing Alex, she'll find a way to fire it at Wyatt."

"You two are giving me too much credit, you know that, don't you?" Alex asked, looking from one sister to the other. "Besides, I don't need bullets. There are other ways to exact revenge if that was what I was after." The corners of her mouth curved ever so slightly, making her words sound more foreboding.

"Alex," Stevi warned. "You're supposed to be on your best behavior, remember?" Leaning in toward her, she added quietly,

"Especially during the reception, with all these people around."

"Me?" Alex asked innocently, splaying her hand across her chest.

"Shocked?"

"Didn't you know? I'm *always* on my best behavior," Alex said with a wink.

"Heaven help us," Stevi declared with a long, weary sigh.

Alex smiled as she heard her sisters both groan behind her as she walked away.

CHAPTER THIRTEEN

ALEX HAD NO SOONER walked away from
Andy and Stevi than she saw Dorothy making her way around the outer fringes of the
reception very slowly. From where Alex
was standing, the housekeeper appeared
to be scanning the crowd, her round face
stamped with a look of concern. Alex could
read it even at a distance.

Whatever it was, she didn't want her father being bothered with it. He had enough
to deal with just getting through this funeral. Though he tried to keep up appear-
ances, she could see that Uncle Dan's death
had really hit him extremely hard. She
didn't want anything else heaped on his
shoulders.

The bite to eat she'd promised herself
was going to have to wait a little longer,
Alex decided.

Turning, she headed away from the buffet tables, picking up her pace as she wove her way through the clusters of people who had come to say their final farewell to Uncle Dan.

Raising her hand over her head as she got closer to the housekeeper, Alex called out her name and waved.

Dorothy heard her before she saw her. Alex could see her cock her head.

"Dorothy, over here!" Alex cried.

Dorothy saw her and appeared immensely relieved. She quickly hurried over.

Alex took hold of the woman's hands when they reached each other. "You look like you just got a call from the IRS saying we forgot to pay our taxes for the last five years and they're going to be taking the inn away from us."

The worst-case scenario took the older woman aback. "Well, it's not *that* bad," she admitted.

Alex flashed the housekeeper a bright smile. "Good, then we'll handle it, whatever it is. Now, what's up?" she asked, slipping her arm around the woman's wide shoulders.

"It's Ms. Carlyle," she confided. At a spry ninety-five, Anne Josephine Carlyle was the inn's oldest guest, hands down. She was also, as of a couple of years ago, their only resident guest. "She made several complaints to me about the noise coming from the reception and just now. She told me she would be in her room, packing. She said that if she wanted to endure this kind of noise, she would have just stayed in her old apartment complex instead of moving in here."

Alex suppressed a sigh. She needed to nip this in the bud before it got out of hand. She started heading toward the inn. "And you say she's packing?"

"That's what she said when she left the dining room," Dorothy told her as she quickened her pace to keep up. Alex hurried up the back steps to the veranda, heading for the inn's back door. "I tried to talk to her, to explain about poor Mr. Dan, but she didn't seem to want to listen. She completely shut me out," Dorothy told her. "I tried, Miss Alex, I really did."

The fact that Dorothy felt she'd failed to change the older woman's mind left her visibly disheartened.

"I know you did," Alex assured her as they walked in together. "This isn't your fault, Dorothy. I guess when you turn ninety-five, you feel like you've earned the right to have a few things your way."

Anne Carlyle had been coming to the inn long before Alex's father had taken over the management of the place from her late grandfather, Kent.

Initially, the retired fifth-grade teacher spent a couple of weeks at the inn every summer. The rest of the time, she and a group of her friends, all teachers and all either widowed, divorced or never married, would select a different European country to visit and they would go on vacation there together.

But as time passed and her group of friends grew smaller and smaller by attrition, Ms. Carlyle spent more and more of her summers at the inn. She believed the stretch of sand by the point reminded her a little of the Riviera.

Eventually, as her mobility became an issue and the former avid hiker needed a cane, the elementary school teacher stopped traveling abroad altogether. Retirement and advanced age, plus a healthy inheritance left to her by her mother, eventually saw the woman setting up permanent residence at Ladera-by-the-Sea.

Alex's father had placed her in the Queen Mary Room. It was on the ground floor, part of the original inn, although it, along with the other original rooms, had been remodeled twice. And, most importantly, Anne Carlyle's room was located just off the dining room, only requiring her to make a short walk for her meals.

Arrangements had been made when she finally moved in for her monthly rate, lower than other guests, to include three meals. Alex's father had managed to assuage the woman's pride by saying she was eligible for a discount since she was staying at the inn year-round.

Right now, she doubted Ms. Carlyle

was actually going to carry out her threat and leave, but she knew the woman probably wanted to be talked into staying. This rather flimsy reason to vent her displeasure was more likely a ploy to get someone to tell her that she mattered.

Reaching her door, Alex told Dorothy she would handle it from here.

The housekeeper looked at her uncertainly. "You're sure?" she asked.

"I'll be fine," Alex assured her.

Dorothy inclined her head, accepting the decision. "Call if you need me."

"Don't I always?" Alex smiled.

She waited until the housekeeper was gone before knocking quietly on the former teacher's door.

"Ms. Carlyle?" Alex raised her voice, aware that the woman was a little hard of hearing. "It's Alex. May I come in, please? I'd like to talk with you."

In response, Alex heard shuffling on the other side of the door. But the petite woman didn't open to her. "I'm busy packing. What do you want?"

"It's about the packing," Alex acknowledged. "I'd like to apologize for all the noise today."

There was no reply. Alex stood there, silently counting off numbers in her head. She was going to give the woman to the count of one hundred before she tried to knock again.

The door opened just as she reached eighty-three.

The slender, gray-haired woman, who looked remarkably years younger than the date on her birth certificate, looked at her through rimless glasses. Her sharp, gray eyes missed nothing.

"I find it very disturbing, you know," Ms. Carlyle finally said in a crisp voice. "All this noise. I can't hear myself think."

"I am truly sorry about that," Alex replied, carefully sitting next to the suitcase. "It should be over soon. You're more than welcome to attend." Although she was certain nothing escaped Ms. Carlyle's attention, she pretended the former teacher hadn't heard about the reason for the gathering by the ocean. "It's a funeral reception for one of our longtime recurring guests. Daniel Taylor."

The woman made no comment. Maybe she hadn't attended either the service or the reception because she might have felt she didn't know Wyatt's father. "He'd been coming here every summer for the past thirty years. For the past twenty-one, he always brought his son, Wyatt, with him. I'm sure you must have met him at one time or—"

Ms. Carlyle waved away the rest of her words. "Yes, yes, I met him."

"You didn't like him?" Alex asked, coming to the only conclusion she could think of.

This time the narrow shoulders rose and fell in a vague shrug as Ms. Carlyle leaned heavily on her cane, using both hands. The next moment, she'd made a U-turn and was making her way back to the open suitcase spread out on her bed. "I liked him well enough."

"All right, then," Alex said slowly, feeling her way around the words she was about to say very carefully. The old woman, in her own way, was as much of a fixture at the inn as the wraparound veranda. "Then you'll let me bring you to the reception?"

"No, I most certainly will not," Ms. Carlyle declared firmly.

The most direct path between two points had always been, and would continue to be, a straight line. Alex didn't bother meandering. "Mind if I ask why?"

Blessed, even at her age, with flawless skin, the former teacher raised her chin and announced, "I don't do funerals."

The sentence hung in the air for several moments and then the woman relented and explained her abrupt statement. "Too many of my friends have passed these last few years. Funerals just serve to remind me all over again that they're gone. I don't like being reminded how alone I am these days."

Alex put her hand over the woman's, squeezing ever so lightly. "You're not alone, Ms. Carlyle. We're all here for you at the inn."

Ms. Carlyle sniffed, but Alex had a feeling she was waiting to be convinced.

Wanted to be convinced. "You're just saying that because I'm a paying guest here."

Alex inclined her head until she made eye contact. "You know better than that."

The older woman sniffed again. "Maybe I do, maybe I don't," she conceded loftily.

"C'mon," Alex coaxed, getting off the bed. "Let me take you. Cris spent all morning getting the buffet ready. You like her cooking—you told me so."

"I know what I like and what I don't like, Alexandra," Ms. Carlyle snapped. "I'm not senile."

Alex had never seen the woman so defensive before.

"No ma'am," Alex said, deliberately sounding contrite.

The thinly penciled-in brows rose. "And don't think I don't know what you're doing, trying to appeal to me by acting meek and chastised." She gave Alex a stern look. "I know you, girl, you've got far too much spirit to be meek—but I do appreciate the gesture." She sighed, lowering her defensive wall a bit. "I'd feel like an old fossil out there."

"Not possible," Alex assured her. "You are just about the youngest woman I know."

The woman laughed dismissively. "Well, now you're serving up a tray full of baloney."

"No baloney," Alex replied. "Just the truth." She glanced through the window that was facing the ocean—and the guests at the reception. Was it her imagination or was the crowd thinning out? "The reception should be over soon," she promised. "Try to hang on until then, can you do that?"

Ms. Carlyle did her best to grumble and look put out. "I suppose so, yes."

"Great," Alex declared warmly. "Because we'd all miss you something awful if you moved out."

"I'm not going anywhere," Ms. Carlyle said, abruptly doing an about-face. "You clearly need someone around who can teach you grammar."

"Whatever it takes to make you stay." Alex hoped she wouldn't end up with English lessons after this. "You're more a part of this inn than we are." The moment Alex said it, an idea occurred to her.

Ms. Carlyle looked at her, concerned. "What's wrong, Alexandra?"

"Nothing," she replied slowly as she reviewed her idea. "It's just that I've suddenly realized you've been here a long time."

"Yes, I know," Ms. Carlyle acknowledged guardedly, never taking her eyes off Alex. "Does that mean you want to raise my monthly rate?"

Alex bit her lip to stop from smiling. "No, definitely not. Your rates are still exactly the same. But it occurs to me that you could be of great service to someone I know."

Looking a little bewildered, Ms. Carlyle said, "My dear, I haven't socialized with members of the opposite gender for a very long time. I take it you're trying to set me up with someone, correct? I have no idea how you came under this false impression that I'd be interested."

Alex pressed her lips together. She didn't want to offend the woman by laughing at the very idea that she could possibly be setting her up.

"No, this isn't any kind of a social setup. Let me start over, please," she requested, afraid the laugh bubbling up in her throat was going to escape. "At the time of his death, Daniel Taylor was working on a book about the history of the inn. When he realized he only had a little time left, he asked his son to finish writing the book for him." And Anne Carlyle was a treasure trove of stories about the inn's past. The best part was that if Wyatt was busy getting his information from the older woman, he wouldn't have to get in her way. She would be free to run the inn.

Ms. Carlyle would feel useful, sharing her past in a manner of speaking, and Alex wouldn't have to spend hours talking to Wyatt.

It was a win-win situation.

"You would be doing everyone a huge service if you allowed him to interview you," she told the reluctant woman. "I'm sure you have some very colorful stories to share."

Ms. Carlyle looked at her thoughtfully. "Well, I suppose it can't do any harm to talk to him. Daniel Taylor," she repeated. "He was that reporter, wasn't he?" she asked. "The one who came here every first of July. He had that gangly boy with him most of the time, didn't he?"

"*All* of the time in the summers," Alex corrected her. "And as for Wyatt, he was gangly at one point. He's filled out some since then. So, what do you say, Ms. Carlyle? Will you do it?"

"I suppose it wouldn't do any harm," she repeated, less reluctantly than before.

"Wyatt will work around you," Alex promised. "He can interview you whenever you feel is convenient. And, if during the session you get too tired, he'll—"

"Why should I be too tired?" Ms. Carlyle intoned. "I'm not *that* old."

"No, ma'am, you're not," Alex readily agreed. She took a breath, then asked the next logical question. "So then you'll stay on at the inn?"

The former teacher liked, on occasion, engaging in drama. "Well, if I must, I must.

It is, after all, for the good of the inn—
might help your father get a little more
business in the off-season.

"It might, at that," Alex agreed. "Thank
you." She leaned over and brushed her
lips against the other woman's paper-thin
cheek.

Ms. Carlyle moved her head back, waving her away. "Don't get all sentimental on
me now, girl," she ordered.

But Alex could tell by the sparkle in her
eyes that Anne Carlyle really did like the
display of affection.

"Let me bring him to you," Alex said,
prepared to drag Wyatt back here if necessary. "Then you two can work out the
details."

"A lady does not entertain men in her
room, my dear. I will meet Mr. Taylor's
son in the parlor, by the reception desk."

"As you wish, Ms. Carlyle," Alex said.
Standing beside her, she presented the
crook of her elbow to the woman.

Ms. Carlyle slipped her hand through the
offered arm. "If you would be kind enough
to ask Dorothea to unpack for me and put

my clothes away into the closet and chest of drawers, I would be grateful."

"Consider it done," Alex promised.

"I will consider it done when it is actually done, not before." The older woman had always insisted that words were tools and their meaning should be taken quite literally.

Alex knew a losing argument when she saw one. "Of course," she said, conceding the battle to Ms. Carlyle. For now.

CHAPTER FOURTEEN

EVER SINCE SHE could remember, even when she was exhausted, Alex found she always had hidden reserves of energy she could tap into. If she dug deep enough.

She had no desire to leave Anne Carlyle far behind her in her dust, or to make the woman feel her age, but there was no way Ms. Carlyle could possibly keep up to her normal pace.

Alex had to walk in slow motion. It wasn't easy for a type-A personality like her, but she focused on the promise that by bringing Wyatt and Ms. Carlyle together this way, she would be killing a number of birds with one large, flat rock. Wyatt would have another rich source of history for the book he was writing, Ms. Carlyle would feel useful and enjoy the respect coming her way and it would certainly take the burden off her, at least for a while.

And there was always the chance that, after interviewing Ms. Carlyle and talking with her father, plus combining that with his own father's notes and partial draft, Wyatt wouldn't need to spend any time with her at all.

That was a good thing, she told herself. For some reason, she didn't feel heartened.

"Alexandra."

The sharp, authoritative tone made her turn her head. Ms. Carlyle had fallen a few steps behind and appeared far from happy about it.

Alex quickly doubled back. "Sorry," she apologized with feeling. "I got lost in thought."

Deep gray eyes narrowed as they took measure of the young woman in front of her.

"Apparently. Perhaps we should do this some other time," Ms. Carlyle suggested. Anyone could see that she was more than willing to turn around and return to the inn and her room.

No, no. She needed to at least set this up now. "I have a better idea. Why don't you sit here on the veranda and I'll go find Wyatt and bring him back to you?"

Ms. Carlyle looked skeptically at the white wicker chair that was placed just so against the inn's back wall. "I suppose I could wait a little while," she conceded. "As long as you don't take too long."

"I'll bring him right back the moment I find him," Alex promised.

Leaning heavily on her cane, the angular woman lowered herself into the wicker chair. Once firmly planted, she looked up at Alex. "Well, what are you waiting for?"

"Not a thing," Alex replied half a second before she took off.

It took her longer to locate Wyatt than she was happy about. Acutely aware that Anne Carlyle was not the most patient of women, Alex cut through the crowd and grabbed Wyatt by the hand the moment she spotted him.

He was standing in the middle of a group of people—mostly women—his own age.

Admirers of his father? Or were they *Wyatt's* friends?

She told herself it didn't matter and that there was no reason for her to feel that quickening of her pulse. What Wyatt did and who he did it with was no concern of hers, especially once this day was behind them.

It still felt good to detach him from the semicircle of mostly women, though.

"C'mon, Wyatt," Alex declared, leaving no room for him to protest. "I need you."

Wyatt looked at her, somewhat stunned. "Now there's something I never thought I'd live to hear," he told her as he allowed himself to be extracted from the group and pulled along the grounds. "Where are you taking me? Not that it really matters," he tacked on glibly. "Somewhere private to have your way with me?"

The wisecrack almost caused Alex to stumble. She shot him a look over her shoulder, hoping it came across as sufficiently annoyed. The man was simply impossible.

"It's not like that, you idiot," she retorted. "Ms. Carlyle is waiting to talk with you."

"Ms. Carlyle." He rolled the name over in his head as they headed toward the inn. "You mean, that woman with a cane who keeps to herself?" he asked.

Before Ms. Carlyle had become a permanent guest at the inn, she would always arrive the last week of summer while Wyatt and his father would spend the first month of the summer there, so their paths hadn't initially crossed. However, once the inn became the retired teacher's address, it would have been impossible for Wyatt not to at least be aware of the woman.

"That's her. And I think you're really going to want to talk to her. She's been keeping a lot more to herself than you think," Alex said, her excitement mounting despite her attempt to remain neutral, at least around Wyatt.

"How's that again?" Wyatt asked. Alex had always had the ability to confound him and leave him puzzled more than anyone else he'd ever known. Now was certainly no exception.

Alex turned toward Wyatt for a split second, talking fast. She could see that Ms. Carlyle was still seated, but that, she was well aware, was subject to change at any moment.

"Anne Carlyle has been coming to the inn for over sixty-five years. She's seen a great many changes here, not to mention a lot of famous people. The woman undoubtedly has hundreds of stories you could coax out of her with that Hollywood-honed charm of yours."

"Hollywood-honed charm," he echoed, amused. "Is that a compliment or a put-down, Alex?" He addressed the question to the back of her head as she continued to pull him in her wake. Each time he matched her pace, she sped up.

"You decide," she said without turning around. She wasn't about to let him see her smile. "She's tired now because it's late in the day, but you and she can made arrangements as to when would be the best time for you to conduct the interviews. I promise you, you won't be sorry."

Wyatt surprised her by suddenly pulling back, bringing her to an abrupt halt.

"What?" she demanded.

Ms. Carlyle was an old woman and he could easily track her down if she left the veranda. Right now, he needed to satisfy his curiosity. "Why are you doing this for me?"

For a moment she just looked at him— and then she pulled her hand away. The fact that her pulse had escalated again both bothered and annoyed her. Why couldn't he just accepted this as a good deed and be done with it? Why did he feel the need to put everything she did under a microscope?

"Because Ms. Carlyle needs to feel her days have some sort of purpose to them, and because the sooner you get your information and finish the book, the faster you'll be out of here—and out of my hair," she retorted.

That sounded more like the Alex he knew. "Oh, so this is about you and your hair?" he said, deadpan.

"Something like that," she answered curtly.

With that, she made a beeline for the back stairs. Curbing her desire to take them two at a time, Alex still hurried, going up the steps quickly.

"I found him, Ms. Carlyle," she announced.

"I can see that," Ms. Carlyle replied crisply. "I'm not blind, girl."

"I didn't mean to imply that you were," Alex replied politely. "Wyatt, this is the lady I've been telling you about, Ms. Anne Josephine Carlyle. Ms. Carlyle, this is Wyatt Taylor. He's the one—"

"I know who he is," the woman snapped, cutting her off. "He's been coming to the inn for quite a while now." Her gray eyes narrowed as she took slow measure of the man beside Alex. "My condolences on the loss of your father. He seemed like a very nice young man."

Wyatt suppressed a smile. He supposed to someone Ms. Carlyle's age, his father would have seemed young.

"Thank you. He was. May I sit?" He nodded at the chair beside hers.

A small smile graced the woman's thin lips. "I can't see why not. Go ahead."

Wyatt took his seat.

Alex could see he was already working his charm on the former teacher.

She supposed that he might have been able to do the same with her if she hadn't been so vigilantly on her guard since childhood. Since around the time she realized her father and Wyatt were bonding.

That was when Uncle Dan's skinny, waiflike, teasing son officially became the enemy in her eyes. Up until that time, she'd had a crush on him. But, from then on, her mission in life became to show him up whenever she could.

"Tomorrow morning, then, at eight," Wyatt was saying. Rising, he took Ms. Carlyle's hand in his and brought it to his lips, lightly kissing it in the time-honored European fashion. "I'm looking forward to it."

For just for a moment Alex saw the crusty woman melt and transform into a schoolgirl.

A delicate laugh escaped the woman's lips and she replied, "As am I, Mr. Taylor."

Bowing ever so slightly, Wyatt said, "Wyatt, please. And thank you." To Alex he said, "And thank you, Alex, for bringing Ms. Carlyle to my attention."

Because they had an audience, Alex couldn't say what she wanted to say to him. Instead, she was forced to return Wyatt's smile and murmur, "My pleasure."

Wyatt's smile told her he knew she was lying through her teeth and that pleasure was the farthest emotion from what she was feeling.

Ms. Carlyle leaned forward, one hand on top of the other on her cane for support as well as leverage.

Wyatt deliberately extended the crook of his arm before Alex had a chance to move.

"Allow me," he said.

Ms. Carlyle immediately slipped her arm through his.

Yup, Alex thought, he had definitely charmed the woman—and in less than five minutes, at that. Apparently advanced age was not an automatic Wyatt immunity.

Moving ahead of the slow procession, Alex held the back door open for them.

"Thank you, Alex," he said as he and Ms. Carlyle crossed the threshold and made their way inside.

Alex had the impression that in this little drama that was unfolding, *he* thought that she was playing the part of the lowly servant.

And so did she.

What *was* it about this man that always made her feel inadequate and lacking and desperately needing to compensate?

Alex let the door close behind her just in time to hear Wyatt ask, "Now, which way do I go to reach your room, Ms. Carlyle?"

Given the woman's previous comment about men in her bedroom, Alex fully expected to hear her tell Wyatt she could very well take it from here.

Instead, she heard the woman laugh. *Nervously.* "It's right down that corridor, Wyatt. Next to the dining hall."

He was good, Alex thought grudgingly, she had to give him that. But there was absolutely no way she would ever tell him so, not without a great deal of torture first.

Alex left them and headed over to the reception desk to relieve poor Dorothy.

"Thanks for minding the store. Anything happen I should know about?"

Dorothy shook her head. "I think almost everyone staying at the inn is still at the reception. Oh, except for your friend, Tracy."

"Stacy," Alex corrected her. "What about her?"

"I saw her come in and then go out again. She was all dressed up. Glittery, even," Dorothy tacked on.

Alex smiled, nodding. "She was probably going out on a date. She likes to cram as much living as she can into any given amount of time. According to her, it makes up for working like a driven person the rest of the time." Alex said the last part more to herself than to the woman who had just vacated the desk. "Nothing else?" Alex asked.

The housekeeper shook her head. "Nope. It's been as quiet as a church on Monday morning," she reported dutifully.

"Sounds good. Thanks again—and I'd turn in early tonight if I were you. Half the guests will be checking out tomorrow morning. There'll be lots of rooms to straighten up."

"Best feeling in the world, being busy."

Dorothy had left her alone less than ninety seconds before she saw Wyatt walking over to her desk.

Now what? she wondered.

"Something I can help you with?" she asked, thinking it best to take the offensive when it came to Wyatt.

He didn't say yes, and he didn't say no. What he did say was, "You do continue to surprise me, Alex," making her wonder what he meant by that and if he was being sarcastic, or if his comment was actually genuine.

"Not that a woman doesn't like to hear that she's keeping a man on his toes, but why's that?"

"Because you've been acting so nice to me these past three days."

And you're making me regret it. You really are. "At the risk of stating the obvious—your father died. Kicking you down a well doesn't really seem appropriate at a time like this. Maybe next week," she added.

Wyatt wasn't ready to let the matter go just yet. "That explains why you were being nice to me before the funeral and maybe it even explains why you were being nice to me during the reception. But talking Ms. Carlyle into interview sessions has nothing to do with my father dying."

She lifted one shoulder in a careless half shrug. "Well, not his dying, but this book you're going to be finishing up is really *his* book if you think about it, so I'm really just being nice to Uncle Dan—*not* you."

His eyes held hers. "I think there's more to it than that."

It was true what they said. No good deed ever went unpunished.

"Oh?"

"Yes," Wyatt answered, his tone soft but unwavering. "I think despite everything you say, deep down inside you really like me."

His conclusion, said out loud and out of the blue that way, left her speechless. Not exactly a routine occurrence for her.

It took her more than a second to find her tongue and longer than that to find her wits.

"Well…then…it must be *really* deep down, because I'm not aware of it…. Now, if you don't mind, I've got the inn's monthly accounts to go over."

And with that, she proceeded to completely ignore him.

Or at least to act as if she did.

It was a little, she thought when Wyatt finally walked away, like trying to ignore air. It wasn't exactly possible.

CHAPTER FIFTEEN

THE RECEPTION LASTED as long as it lasted.

After all, Alex reasoned, it was a gathering of Uncle Dan's friends, paying tribute and their last respects to a man they had all held in high regard. A man who, from the bits and pieces of the conversations she'd picked up after the funeral, had enriched every life he came in contact with, every life he ever touched.

How could you hope to contain that within an hour, or two or three?

By the time everyone had finally left, the sky had grown dark and the day was gone. Even the crashing of the ocean's waves seemed to have died down to a gentle lapping.

Cris and Rosemary and a few others had cleared away all the leftovers.

There was a great deal still to be done.

And there was no one around but her.

She'd told Dorothy that she was free for the evening and her sisters had scattered. Cris had taken Ricky to bed and, Alex had no doubt, had taken herself there, as well. Between her regular meals and the food for the reception, Cris had put in an extraordinarily long day and was justifiably wiped out.

As for Stevi and Andy, heaven only knew where they'd gone after the reception.

That left her.

Alex surveyed the grounds, feeling a little overwhelmed. She supposed she could always just call it a night, go back inside and tackle all this in the morning. Heaven knew it would all still be here in the morning.

But Alex had never been the type to put anything off. She liked getting things out of the way when she had the chance, since "later" might come packed with its own set of problems.

Squaring her shoulders, Alex pulled out

a large garbage bag from the box she'd brought with her. *Time to get started.*

She had only filled the bag a third of the way when her father came up behind her.

Considering how he had to feel right now, he didn't look that bad, she consoled herself as she breathed a sigh of relief.

"Can I help you with something, Dad?" she asked, doing her best to sound upbeat.

It didn't seem to be helping because he replied, "I feel bad."

Letting the plastic bag drop, she slipped her arm around his back. "Well, we know it's going to take a long while before—"

Richard stopped his daughter before she could get any further. "No, I mean about today, about what you wound up having to do. I feel bad that I just put this all on your shoulders—the arrangements, the reception, coordinating the guests, the music, the minister—"

It was her turn to interrupt him. "Dad, you did take care of some of it, and so did the girls. And Wyatt, too. It's not like I'm some superhero, doing everything at once. That being said, I wanted to take the burden off you as much as I possibly could. Uncle Dan's passing was a huge shock to all of us, but most of all to you—"

Her father laughed softly. "I think Wyatt might have a difference of opinion on that." Bending over the box on the ground, he extracted another garbage bag, then shook it open.

Alex deliberately took the bag out of his hands, giving him a reproving look.

"Okay," she responded, referring to his last statement, "but I've got a feeling Wyatt will bounce back just fine. And so will you," she added quickly.

Richard hugged her to him, a sad smile curving his mouth. "Tell me, how did you get to be so wise?"

Her eyes crinkled at the corners as she smiled up at him. "I had a great teacher." She brushed a kiss against his cheek. "Now do me a really big favor? Go to bed and get some rest. You've had a long, heart-wrenching day and I have a feeling you didn't get much sleep last night—or the night before that."

"Still, I hate leaving all this to you."

"I'm just going to make a small dent," she assured him. "Besides, I'm the compulsive one, remember?" she asked, tossing his own words back at him.

Richard laughed, shaking his head. "You're never going to let me live that down, are you?"

Alex pretended to consider his question seriously, then gave him half a shrug.

"Maybe someday," she quipped. "Now go, before I call Dorothy down and sic her on you. The woman is strong enough to carry you to your room."

"She might be, at that," he conceded. "But you forget—Dorothy's loyal to me."

"Exactly," she said pointedly. Her grin was wide and confident. "And she wouldn't want you tiring yourself out."

Richard shook his head again, amused as he gave up the fight. "You're just like your mother, you know that? Stubborn to a fault."

Alex all but beamed at the comparison before she went back to gathering the trash. "I consider that a great compliment."

"I meant it to be." Richard took a few

steps toward the inn, then stopped to caution her, "Don't stay out here too long."

"Yes, Dad," Alex agreed dutifully.

Having sent her father on his way, Alex continued gathering the used utensils and plates discarded on any flat surface that was handy. She'd deliberately gotten heavy-duty plastic utensils and plates so that they could be thrown away, but she'd assumed that they would have all made it into the receptacles that had been scattered around the grounds.

So much for assumptions, Alex thought philosophically.

Having gotten a second—or more accurately, a third wind—Alex decided that she'd just keep at it until she ran out of energy—or trash, although the former was far more likely than the latter.

That would leave less for the others to clean up tomorrow.

She supposed her father was right. She was obsessive. But at least it was for a good cause.

Hearing a noise behind her, Alex frowned. Did she have to physically escort her father to his room before she could finally make him get the rest he so badly needed?

"What did I tell you about going to bed?" she asked, pushing an armload of paper plates into a new garbage bag. "What does it take to get you to go? Am I going to have to sing you a lullaby?"

"Might be interesting."

Alex swallowed a startled gasp as her brain registered the fact that the voice was too deep to belong to her father. She swung around.

Wyatt.

She took in a deep breath, trying to steady her nerves.

"What are you doing here?" she asked.

Crossing the rest of the distance to her, Wyatt bent to pick up the trash she'd dropped. He remained crouched, stuffing it into the garbage bag.

And then he looked up at her, the face of innocence. "I'm staying at the inn."

Alex closed her eyes for a second, searching for patience as well as strength. Wyatt had a way of completely evaporating both just by opening his mouth.

"I *know* that," she enunciated slowly, "but I thought you had gone to bed. It's late," she pointed out needlessly.

"I haven't had a curfew for fifteen years."

"Everyone else has gone to bed, so I just thought—"

She stopped abruptly. Why was she even bothering to explain? He was trying to bait her, the way he always had. Some things, no matter what, never changed. In an odd sort of way, she supposed that was comforting.

Or maybe she was just overtired, she amended.

"Never mind. Forget I said anything." Yanking the garbage bag out of his hand, she turned her back on him and got back to work.

Wyatt looked around. "Nobody else out here to help you?"

Why was he still here? She'd been nice to him for most of three days. Didn't that earn her a little payback?

"I already said that everyone else has gone to bed." She looked at him over her shoulder. "I could reenact that with hand puppets if it would help you understand."

Wyatt looked amused. "Might be entertaining, at that," he replied. "Maybe later," he told her, as if the idea was worth considering.

Was he just going to stand there all night watching her? She pressed her lips together. Maybe he'd get bored and leave.

And this odd shiver that was dancing up and down her spine would fade away.

Alex worked her way back toward the rental tent. Unfortunately, she was getting herself worked up faster than she was collecting trash.

She felt his eyes boring into her as he watched her work.

Unable to stand it any longer, she swung around to give Wyatt a piece of her mind.

The hot words on her tongue vanished as she realized he wasn't standing idly by, watching her. He wasn't standing at all. Wyatt had taken one of the bags she'd brought out and was picking up debris on the far side of the tent.

"What are you doing?" she called out

sharply. Alex held everything that Wyatt did suspect, always assuming that he had to have some sort of hidden agenda.

If he noticed her less-than-friendly tone, he gave no indication. "You looked like you were having so much fun, I thought I'd join in."

A retort hovered on her lips, but Wyatt actually looked as if he meant it—not the part about it being fun, but that he wanted to help her clean up. She supposed it wouldn't hurt to give him the benefit of the doubt this one time.

"You don't have to," she told him primly. Wyatt being sarcastic or cynical, she knew how to handle. Wyatt behaving thoughtfully threw her for a loop.

"Yeah, I know. But then, neither did you."

"It's my inn," she pointed out, then waited for him to get picayune and point out that, technically, it wasn't hers but her father's. That was the sort of thing that Wyatt did.

Except that he didn't this time.

"It was my father." That said a great deal without really saying a word directly.

The silence between them, even after only a minute, felt far too pregnant for her to allow it to continue.

"It was a nice service."

But even as she said it, there was a part of her that was braced for some sort of a challenge from Wyatt. After having been subjected to years of contradictions, the anticipation wasn't something that would go away easily.

"Yeah, it was," Wyatt agreed, then, with a touch of wistfulness and more than a little contained sorrow. "Dad would have liked it. It had just the right tone to it."

Wyatt added, "You found the right man to preside over the service."

The minister and Dan had known each other fairly well. The two men had gotten along, finding shared philosophies.

Alex smiled, remembering being privy for some of the conversations that had involved the two men and her father.

"Uncle Dan didn't wear his religion on his sleeve, didn't really talk about it at all, but I got the sense that deep down, he believed in something outside of himself."

"He did." Wyatt worked his way closer to Alex. "When I was a kid, he once told my mother that the meaning of Christmas had gotten lost in the commercialism. I extrapolated a lot from that."

That fit with the studious bookworm she remembered. She'd been the tomboy, he'd been the student. "How old were you?"

"Old enough not to believe in Santa Claus anymore."

She laughed shortly. "I thought you were born that way."

He wasn't sure just what she meant by that. He would have thought that for once, they had gotten past hard feelings.

"What way?" he asked cautiously.

"Cynical," she said. "Not believing in things."

He paused. He was close enough to her to be able to see every nuance of her features.

Close enough to appreciate the way the moonlight highlighted her hair and the contours of her face.

Close enough to detect the light fragrance she always wore.

For a moment there was only the sound of crickets. They seemed to be spread out all through the grounds, hidden from view and calling out to their potential mates. Their sound seemed to imitate the beat of his pulse.

"I believe in a lot of things," he told her quietly, his eyes on hers. "Just not in portly old men sliding down chimneys, dragging down sacks of toys in their wake, or in rabbits hopping around with baskets filled with foil-wrapped chocolate eggs and candy corn."

"You left out the Tooth Fairy," she said wryly.

"You mean, she's not real?"

And then she began to laugh. Really laugh.

It blended rather harmoniously with the sound of his laughter.

CHAPTER SIXTEEN

A FEW SECONDS LATER, their laughter faded, slowly disappearing into the night.

The tidal wave in the pit of Alex's stomach did not.

She found it difficult to take a deep breath. Difficult to think of anything except for how the distance between them seemed to have evaporated and how close Wyatt was to her.

It was difficult for her to think at all.

And then, for one long frozen moment in time, she was certain Wyatt was going to kiss her.

Alex upbraided herself for not moving, for not doing something to prevent it—and upbraided herself even more for wanting it to happen.

When it didn't—when Wyatt *didn't* kiss her—she no longer knew *how* to feel. All she knew was that she'd lost her crutch, lost having something she could blame for this shift within her. If Wyatt had kissed her, then she could have blamed the rise in her body temperature on embarrassment, not longing.

Now there was only embarrassment because for that single moment in time, she'd longed to have him kiss her.

He wanted to kiss her.

Wyatt struggled to tamp down the urge. Again.

Because he sensed that, just as he had the last time, if he did kiss Alex, things would not go down well between them. He knew her. She'd say something flippant and cutting, or turn her head, presenting him with a mouthful of blond hair at the last moment.

Or worse, she could show displeasure and disdain after.

He didn't have an ego the way Alex had repeatedly accused him of having over the years, but what he did have was pride. Pride that did not wear humiliation very well. He didn't want to risk having her humiliate him.

He knew how to read other women's signals, other women's vibes. But though he'd known Alex longer than he'd known any other woman in his life, he just couldn't read her. He had never quite been able to figure out what was going on in her head. Alex had always been, and most likely would always be, an enigma for him.

So Wyatt backed away, suppressing the very real, very strong desire to brush his lips against hers, to hold her in his arms for some reason other than to restrain her from taking a swing at him.

Getting himself back under control, he took a breath, then said, nodding at the garbage bag he'd dropped at his feet, "I'd better get back to work."

"I was just going to suggest you go on inside." Alex slowly looked around the grounds. They had managed, in a very short time, to pick up most everything. "We seem to have made a pretty good dent," she attested. Then, looking up at the sky, she added, "And there seems to be a fog rolling in."

Wyatt was amused by the excuse she'd resorted to. The woman was really clutching at straws. Maybe she wouldn't have pulled away if he'd kissed her, at that.

But for now, the moment was gone and he wasn't about to pursue it.

"I thought that was a problem only if you were a ship," he commented.

What was wrong with her? Instead of getting annoyed at what she heard as mockery, she felt her cheeks heating and found herself being grateful for the cover of darkness. Otherwise, he would have seen how very pink her cheeks were becoming. He would have undoubtedly made some comment about that and make a bad situation that much worse.

"If it gets too thick, it hampers visibility," she informed him coolly. "I wouldn't want to stumble over you."

He looked at her for a long moment— as if he knew she was just flailing around, saying the first thing that came to her mind.

What was *wrong* with her? she silently demanded again, exasperated with herself.

"So you're stopping?" Wyatt questioned, his tone saying he didn't believe the excuse she'd just come up with.

She hadn't wanted to, but stopping was better than being out here in the dark with him—feeling more vulnerable than she ever had before. So she reluctantly said, "I'm stopping."

Wyatt inclined his head, his eyes never leaving hers. "Works for me." Garbage bag in hand, he walked over to the back of the tent and deposited it beside the ones that were already there. "I'll see you in the morning," he told her as he walked by her again, toward the inn.

"You'll be seeing Ms. Carlyle in the morning," she corrected him.

That stopped him in his tracks. "And that means what? That I can only see one or the other? Either Ms. Carlyle or you? You're not one and the same person, Alex. I've seen you standing next to the woman, so I know it's possible to see you both."

Growing up, she was the one who was

always able to fluster him. Why—and *how*—had the tables suddenly been turned?

Alex struggled hard, determined not to let him suspect what was going on inside her. If he even suspected that she was anything but the cool, collected image she'd been projecting for most of her life, he'd find a way to taunt her about it. She could help him during his time of grief but she was *not* about to allow him to perceive anything but strength coming from her.

"No, wise guy, what I was saying was that your first interview with Ms. Carlyle will be taking up most of your time tomorrow."

"Maybe so." Though he doubted it. The woman might have come across as feisty, but she was also rather frail. He didn't want to tire her out. Getting information out of her was undoubtedly going to be a long, slow, drawn-out process. But he had a hunch it would be more than worth it. "But that doesn't mean I can't see you, as well, if only hovering around somewhere in the background."

"I *don't* hover," she emphasized. Her expression dared him to say otherwise. "Time to go in," she announced, not wanting the moment to devolve into an exchange of sharp, choice words.

Especially not tonight, not after having laid Uncle Dan to rest earlier in the day. It seemed disrespectful to the man's memory to tell his son he was an opinionated idiot. She'd save that for some future argument since she knew that if Wyatt was anywhere around her, there would definitely be future arguments.

"Funny," Wyatt said, looking directly at her, "I was just thinking the very same thing. Time to go in," he echoed.

Alex realized that her mouth had gone dry and that queasy feeling she'd been experiencing was intensifying rather than abating.

She said nothing as she moved swiftly toward the house.

"So, DO I FINALLY get you all to myself before I have to check out, or is there some planet that needs saving that only you can reach?"

Alex had gotten up early and was having breakfast alone in the dining room. She hadn't expected Stacy to be up yet, let alone dressed.

The woman slid into the chair opposite her. Reaching across the table, Stacy helped herself to Alex's coffee cup and took a sip before putting it back down. "When we were in college together, I had no idea I was associating with a superheroine who bent steel with her bare hands while juggling a thousand details at the same time."

Stacy laughed and shook her head, reaching for the cup again.

"Really, I thought that *my* job kept me hopping." This sip was longer and she paused to relish the hot coffee. "I'm sitting on some island beach sipping mai tais, in comparison to you. How do you do it?" Stacy truly wanted to know. "How do you keep all those balls in the air without dropping one or going crazy?"

Alex shrugged. It wasn't something she actively thought about.

"I just do whatever needs to be done, that's all," she replied. Reclaiming her cup,

Alex took a sip before the coffee was all gone. Then she rose and went to the sideboard where Cris had put out a thermos of coffee to keep it hot. She poured Stacy a cup and topped hers, returning to her seat with them. "And right now, what needs to be done is for the two us to go somewhere, do a little shopping and finally catch up."

Stacy splayed her hand over her chest and pretended to look shocked before grasping the hot mug in her hands. "Do you think the inn can do without you for a few hours?"

"Most definitely," Alex answered without hesitation. "My father all but said he was throwing me out today. I'm all yours." She flashed a smile at her friend. And because she detected a bit of skepticism coming from Stacy, Alex added, "Really," with feeling.

"And what about that hot man?" Stacy asked, dropping her voice a sultry octave or two. "Can *he* do without you, too?"

Alex knew there was absolutely no point in pretending that she *didn't* know who Stacy was talking about, otherwise she would have. But Stacy would only keep coming up with trite adjectives to describe him until she acknowledged Wyatt.

"Wyatt's busy today, doing research."

A rather smoldering expression bordering on wicked came over Stacy's face. "Is that a euphemism for…?"

It was hard to keep from rolling her eyes, but Alex managed to refrain only because Stacy *was* her friend. "That's not a euphemism for anything, Stacy. Wyatt *is* actually doing research today." That he was actually keeping his word to his father was to his credit, not that she would say as much to him. "Right now, he's interviewing Ms. Carlyle."

Alex could see that Stacy's brain was going into overdrive. "Well, if he'd like to interview me next about my stay here, I'd be more than willing to bare my soul to him—and anything else he might want me to bare." Her grin just kept growing. "Seeing as how you said you weren't interested in him," Stacy concluded, looking at her pointedly. "Or are you?"

"What I'm interested in right now," Alex

told her pleasantly, finishing her breakfast, "is spending an afternoon with you. I'm sure we'll need an entire afternoon just to begin to catch up."

Stacy grinned broadly. "Oh, honey, you have *no* idea. Get ready to have your ears talked off."

DESPITE THE FACT that Stacy did monopolize about ninety percent of the conversation that afternoon as well as most of their time together the following day, the time, Alex felt, seemed to go by much too quickly. Before she knew it, it was time for Stacy to check out of the inn and go back home.

"We have to do this again sometime," Stacy told her, lingering at the reception desk. She was waiting for the cab she had called to arrive and take her to the airport. "Except next time, maybe we can do it without the funeral—"

"And without the corporate emergency," Alex added, reminding Stacy that she was the one cutting her vacation even shorter by two days because of the phone call she'd received from her direct supervisor.

"Touché," Stacy conceded. "Still, we did have fun, didn't we?"

It wasn't really a question, but Alex could sense that her friend needed to hear the sentiment reinforced. "We always do," Alex reminded her.

Stacy caught her lower lip between her teeth, hesitating for a moment before she made the next admission. "Truth be told, I kind of envy you."

Alex was caught off guard by that admission.

She would have thought, if anything, Stacy would have said something about feeling sorry for her. She was fairly confident that Stacy perceived her as being stuck, working in a position where the end goal was not advancement and perks.

"Okay, I'm braced," Alex announced. "So, go ahead. Out with it."

"Braced?" Stacy asked, not following her again. "Why?"

"Because," Alex explained patiently, "the Stacy I know and love would have looked at what I do and think of it as more or less a death sentence."

"Good point," Stacy agreed. "But that was before."

"Before?"

Stacy nodded. "Before hopping on a jet at a moment's notice started getting a little old," she admitted. "Before one relationship after another fell through for me because I had to keep breaking dates and backing out of plans because of these last-minute emergency calls to duty I'd receive."

Alex looked down at the guest book between them on the desk, fiddling with the open page.

"Guys are patient only up to a point before they start resenting coming in second behind a career. Meanwhile, you don't have to try to remember what city—or what country—you're in when you wake up in the morning. And you don't have to try to remember what time zone you're in so you can make a call and not disturb the person you're calling. You know that when you wake up, you'll be exactly in the same place you woke up yesterday."

The smile she'd been forcing faded a little from her lips.

"You get to save the day and be told that you did a good job," she added wistfully. "I *saw* the way your father looked at you at the reception. It was all right there in his eyes, how proud he was of you. People depend on you—"

"They depend on you, too," Alex was quick to point out.

"Yes, but when I come through, no one says anything. It's expected of me. I'm *supposed* to come through—and the second I *don't* come through, someone else will be put in my place. If I want to hear praise or gratitude, I have to record it myself and then play it back. There're just no emotional rewards in my line of work."

Alex had never seen her friend quite so down. She didn't want Stacy leaving like this. That was no way to end a vacation, even a "power" vacation.

"That salary of yours has to be a pretty good size," Alex reminded her.

"Oh, it is," Stacy agreed, but it was obviously not enough. "But money doesn't always fill the hole that's inside. Still," she went on, allowing herself to be rallied a little, "I can buy myself some really nice trinkets to soothe the pain."

Alex looked at the gold bracelet Stacy was wearing on her right wrist. The morning sun was reflecting off the bracelet's intricate weave.

"And that is one *really* nice trinket," Alex said appreciatively.

She grinned again. "It is, at that." Leaving her purse on the counter, Stacy rounded the desk and threw her arms around Alex. "We didn't get nearly enough time together," she lamented, hugging Alex as hard as she could.

"Next time."

"Next time," Stacy agreed.

They both knew that if Stacy remained in her present position, "next time" would be a very long time in coming. And when it did, she, Alex, might be up to her neck at the inn.

But Alex firmly believed that promises were good for the soul. They kept a person going.

The sound of a horn broke the still morning air.

"Well, that's my taxi," Stacy announced, releasing Alex. Moving back around to the front of the desk, she grasped the handle of her suitcase.

Alex came around to stand beside her. "Still wish you'd let me drive you to the airport." She looked toward the front door. She could still dismiss the cabbie and take Stacy to the airport herself.

But Stacy shook her head. "You're needed here, Alex. Besides, I really hate to cry in airports. This is much better," she said, pausing a last time to give Alex a final, one-armed hug. "Tell your dad I appreciate the lovely room, but he's never going to make 'Fortune 500' by giving away rooms."

Alex laughed, shaking her head. Her father didn't even own a copy of that magazine, much less read it. "I don't think my dad's really interested in getting into 'Fortune 500,' he just likes extending his own brand of hospitality."

Stacy was a bit more pragmatic in her take on things. "It's harder to be hospitable if there's not enough money to cover the costs of the fresh groceries needed to make breakfast."

"There always will be enough money to cover breakfast," Alex told her with confidence.

"Because you'll see to it," Stacy said knowingly.

"You'd better get out there before the cabbie up and leaves you here."

"Then I'd take you up on your offer to get me to the airport." Stacy grasped the handle of her suitcase one more time. "Make my goodbyes to the rest of your family and tell Dorothy that if she ever gets tired of working at the inn, I've got a place for her with me."

And with that, Stacy hurried out, pulling her suitcase in her wake.

CHAPTER SEVENTEEN

WHEN SHE HAD GOTTEN the two of them together, Alex had assumed that Wyatt's interviews with Ms. Carlyle would last an hour or maybe even two and take a couple of days. Perhaps three.

She *certainly* hadn't believed the woman remembered enough stories for these interviews Wyatt was conducting to continue past a week.

And the sessions didn't just go on for an hour or two. From what she could ascertain, the interviews went on all day long.

Had she not known the circumstances behind the sessions—and the two people involved in them—she would have thought she was witnessing a wealthy dowager vacationing with her much younger paramour. Whenever she ran into Wyatt and Ms. Carlyle in the dining room, on the veranda,

strolling—actually *strolling*—through the
flower gardens that surrounded the front of
the inn, Wyatt appeared to be hanging on
Ms. Carlyle's every word.

She'd known the older woman all of her
life and Alex could *not* recall *ever* seeing
her look so alive.

Initially, Alex had assumed that once
Wyatt had gotten as much information
about the inn's history as he could from
their resident senior citizen, that she would
be next on his list. Although, now she
thought about it, why would she think that
when her dad had more perspective on the
inn to share…? Still, she'd braced herself to
be cornered and followed around for several exceptionally long, excruciating days.

But she'd braced herself each morning
for no reason. Because, from the looks of
it, Wyatt didn't appear to be anywhere near
finished questioning Ms. Carlyle.

After more than a week had gone by,
Alex stopped bracing in anticipation of
meeting with the writer.

Once she'd decided that it was going to
be a while before Wyatt would even get to

her and start picking her brain, Alex was surprised to discover that rather than relief, what she actually felt was an annoying sense of disappointment.

It wasn't as if she was actually looking *forward* to having Wyatt dog her every move, throwing her normal workday into absolute chaos.

No. What she was experiencing, Alex finally decided, was just disappointment that she couldn't put the ordeal behind her yet.

That was her story and she was sticking to it.

And for all intents and purposes, from what she'd picked up as she passed by their table at breakfast this morning—was he taking *all* of his meals with this woman now?—Wyatt and Ms. Carlyle weren't anywhere *near* the home stretch yet.

Which meant that Wyatt was out of her hair.

He hadn't even been *in* her hair yet. That was reason enough for her to be very happy.

So why wasn't she?

Annoyed, Alex deliberately focused her

attention on her regular duties. In addition, she reminded herself that she also had to begin the search for a general contractor. At the very least, the roof had to be repaired.

"Can I help you find something?" Richard asked, addressing the top of Alex's head. She was so completely engrossed in searching through the side drawers of his desk, she mustn't have heard him come in.

Alex was perched on the edge of her dad's custom-ordered office chair. The thing was too comfortable, she lamented. Her mind had wandered again. She wasn't used to this, operating at less than her usual hundred and ten percent.

She cleared her throat as she looked up at him. "I'm looking for that list you said you had. The list of general contractors," she added.

Although her father owned one of the newest computers on the market and that computer was currently sitting on his desk, he rarely used it for more than just a giant, glorified paperweight. He'd always preferred keeping things in physical files he could see and touch rather than ones comprised of megabytes and changeable fonts, existing in the virtual world.

If he couldn't touch it, he couldn't trust it.

"I thought I'd go through the people on that list and find someone to start vetting so that we can get rolling on that addition you want."

He was still standing and looked down at her now. He'd caught something in her voice when she'd said that. "And you don't?"

Alex shrugged, avoiding looking into his eyes. "I didn't say that."

"Sometimes," he told her thoughtfully, "it's what a person doesn't say that's more telling than what she does say." And, he decided, there was no time like the present to straighten things out. "You never told me what you thought about the idea of putting another addition on the inn."

Alex shrugged, still avoiding his eyes. "You never asked me."

He laughed, which caused her to look up quickly. How could she have missed seeing the humor in what she'd just said? "Since when do I have to ask you your opinion on anything?" he demanded, still laughing. "You've always been more than generous about dispensing that opinion before. To anyone with ears."

Alex's mouth curved ever so slightly. "Well, since you asked—"

"I did," he confirmed with a quick nod of his head.

"I don't like things changing," she finally admitted.

Her father smiled. "I already know that," he told her kindly. "But sometimes, things change whether we want them to or not. Take kids, for instance," he said. "The four of you grew up, even though I would have loved to keep those sweet, obedient little girls I had for a while longer."

"We were never obedient," Alex reminded him. "A Mrs. Abernathy, if I recall correctly, once asked you why you were raising four wild Indians."

He remembered the incident. "And I asked her to leave and she did."

"Without paying you." She'd been too

young to remember that on her own, but Uncle Dan had told her that part. Told the story more than once, as well, so that it remained vivid in her mind.

"It was worth it just to get rid of her. No one insulted my girls and got away with it."

"If we hadn't chosen to stay on," Alex said, "who would have helped you with the inn?"

"My point exactly," he declared, leaning forward. "Everything changes, you just have to find the good in that and focus on it, not on the change itself. We need that addition," he told her, then explained why he thought so. "Business has picked up. We've had to turn away people calling in to make reservations."

"Some of them rescheduled."

"And some went to another bed-and-breakfast," he countered. "Every guest we can't accommodate is one we risk losing permanently."

He was right and she knew it. And, she assumed, as with all the other additions, once it was completed, it would look lovely—as long as there were no new, outlandish ideas implemented by an unpredictable contractor like the one she'd fired.

"And that's why I'm here, ready to start vetting them. *If* I ever find that list," she added with just a touch of exasperation. "Where did you put it?"

Rather than say anything, her father crossed to the stand he'd purchased to accommodate the printer.

He opened the drawer that held the extra paper and took out a manila folder. The folder was slightly mangled from the tight fit.

He deposited the folder in the middle of his desk. "I believe this is what you're looking for."

Alex flipped it open. There were several pages of names and addresses plus phone numbers.

"Okay, I'll input all these into the computer—so we won't lose the list," she commented.

"I didn't lose it," he protested. "I knew exactly where it was." His tone told her he was confident she couldn't even begin to challenge him about that.

She sighed. "Okay, so that *I* can always find it easily when I need it. Who knows, I might decide I want a whole bunch of new additions put on the inn." She saw the expression on his face. "Stranger things have happened."

He wasn't about to get into a long discussion over that. Alex had a gift for winning arguments.

"I suppose maybe they have." He deftly switched subjects. "Has Wyatt interviewed you yet about the inn?"

"No. I'm getting the feeling that Ms. Carlyle's got a lot more stories about this inn than I thought. I guess Wyatt must feel as if he struck gold."

Her father nodded. "Then he should be very grateful to you. That was a good idea, getting the two of them together."

Since she hadn't told her father that it was her idea to bring Wyatt together with the woman, and since Ms. Carlyle ordinarily wasn't the type to volunteer information unless specifically asked, Alex was rather surprised that her father knew she was the one who had initially orchestrated the interview sessions.

"Ms. Carlyle told you I brought Wyatt to her?" she asked.

"No," he said. "Wyatt did."

That was even more surprising. She would have *never* thought that Wyatt would give her credit for *anything*.

And then it occurred to her how the topic might have come up. "You asked him how he was doing, didn't you?" she guessed. "And instead of telling you about how he was dealing with his father's death, he started talking about writing the book instead." Alex smiled. That was so typical of him, worrying about the people he cared about. "Wyatt's lucky to have you, Dad. I hope he realizes that."

Richard looked at his firstborn, puzzled by her strange phraseology. "Excuse me?"

"Well, he lost his biological father, but his spare is alive and well," she said. "That has to be comforting to him."

Richard had a feeling that this wasn't just a flippant remark on his daughter's part. It went far deeper than that. He thought he'd already reassured her that she and her sisters came first in his heart and he didn't need a son to fill some missing hole she imagined in his life.

"I care about Wyatt because he's my best friend's son," he said. "I'm not his 'spare' father, Alex. I told you that."

"It's only natural that Wyatt think of you as a spare—a *second*—father if you will," she amended. "And it's all good, because no matter what you said the other day, Wyatt takes the place of the son you cannot deny you've always wanted."

Was she still hung up on that? Just what did it take to convince her that, as intelligent as she was, this time she was dead wrong?

"Alex, I never wanted a son. Certainly not in place of you and your sisters."

"Every man does. Unfortunately, Mom kept popping out girls, so you did the next best thing. You gave us boys' nicknames."

She'd said that to him earlier…. Was that it? Was that where it had started? he wondered. With something so simple and insignificant? And so incorrect? "No, that was your mother's idea," he corrected. "The nicknames were all her idea."

"Mom picked feminine names for us," Alex said. "She told me that."

"That, too." He could see that Alex needed more convincing. "Your mother always liked very feminine-sounding names that lent themselves to boys' nicknames. She got a kick out of it—just be happy I was there to deflect her when she wanted to call you Henri."

Alex rolled the name over in her head and shrugged. "Henri's not bad."

She watched the corners of her father's mouth curve in amusement. "How would you have felt about your teachers calling you Henrietta?"

"Henrietta?" she echoed, cringing. She could just hear what the kids in school would have made out of the name, teasing her mercilessly—until she flattened them. "Thank you for saving me."

Her father grinned and inclined his head. "You're welcome." And then he glanced at the folder, pulling it closer. "Tell you what. I'll go through the list first, narrow it down, then have you complete the vetting on the top three choices. We'll do the interviews together before I sign on with anyone."

Alex was about to say that he didn't have to go through all that, that she could handle it all for him. But she caught herself just in time. She had to remember to curb her tendency to take over like that.

Alex flashed him a smile. "Sounds like a plan to me, Dad."

A WEEK LATER they wound up going with a man who not only had excellent references and who they both could enthusiastically agree on, but the general contractor was also someone who coincidentally met with Cris's approval, as well.

It turned out that the man they hired, Shane McCallister, was also the older brother of one of Cris's friends who she'd gone to school with.

After the deal was finalized and both a fee and a time frame were agreed upon, Richard invited Shane to have lunch with them. He agreed after confiding that he was rather curious to find out just how good a chef Cris had turned out to be.

"Back when she used to hang out with my sister, her idea of preparing a hot meal was having a pizza delivered."

"She's come a long way since then," Richard told him proudly.

Rather than send out one of the inn's employees who doubled as a server during mealtime, Cris brought out the food she'd prepared herself.

The pleased look on Shane's face was not lost on either Alex or her father.

"Why don't you sit down for a few minutes, Cris?" Richard suggested. "Join us."

She begged off. "Can't. But I can bring you my special dessert later."

"Looking forward to it," Shane said.

When Cris returned a little while later, the tray she was carrying held four desserts, not three. Placing one in front of each of them, she took the last one herself and sat at the table with them.

Alex caught her sister watching Shane with hooded eyes to see if he liked her version of Baked Alaska. When he told her as much, saying it with unabashed pleasure in between bites, Cris made no effort to hide the smile that rose to her lips.

"YOU KNOW," ALEX commented after Shane had left and she and her father went back to his office to file away the signed contract, "I don't think I've seen Cris smile like that since…well…since before Mike went into the service."

It had been a long, painful time for her sister. The adjustment to being a widow and a single mom had not been easy for her, even with all the emotional support they'd given her.

Alex looked at her father and added, "I think that hiring Shane might turn out to be not just good for the inn, but good for our resident chef, too."

"That would be an answer to a prayer," her father agreed wholeheartedly, then amended, "Or to at least one of them."

About to leave, Alex stared at her father, trying to understand what he'd just told her. "You've been praying for a man to come in and sweep Cris off her feet?"

"Yes. Why is that so strange?" he asked when he saw the confused look on her face. "Every father wants someone special to come into his little girl's life and take care of her."

But that wasn't what had really caught her attention. Alex narrowed her eyes, hoping she had misunderstood his meaning. "What did you mean by 'to at least one of them'? Just what *else* do you pray for?"

"Health, happiness…" Richard's voice trailed off as he raised his shoulder in a vague shrug. "I'll leave the rest of it up to you to figure out."

She'd already figured it out—and was hoping she was wrong. "Stevi and Andy are too young to get married."

The father in him agreed. "Your mother was younger."

"You don't—" About to protest that times had changed and her sisters were far too young to be as old as her mother had been—in maturity—when something else suddenly hit her. "You…you don't actually mean that you pray for some guy to come stomping in and drag me off with him, do you?"

Richard laughed, shaking his head at the description. That couldn't possibly be Alex's definition of being swept off her feet.

"Definitely not. Those words would never come into any of my prayers," he assured her. And then he paused for a moment, debating whether or not to say anything further. He was still trying to decide when a single word slipped past his lips. "But…"

"But?" Alex echoed.

"*But* I do worry about you. You spend too much of your time working, Alex. You should be out, having fun. Mingling."

It was not an unfamiliar refrain. They'd been through this before—periodically.

"I mingle just fine right here, Dad. And I *am* having fun." She capsulated her life for him, going over all the main elements that were important to her. "Working here at the inn, meeting different people from all walks of life, hanging out with my family, being part of the inn's long history— this is my idea of fun."

Alex glanced at her watch. It was time for her to make a tactical exit before her father came up with anything more.

"So please, stop worrying, Dad." She brushed a quick kiss against his cheek. "My life is good—no, make that *great*," she corrected. "And I have absolutely no complaints."

"But you will, Alex," Richard said quietly as she shut the office door behind her. "Someday, years from now, you will."

And hoping that it would turn out otherwise just wasn't enough.

But all he could do was set things up— which he had.

He crossed his fingers and hoped that things would go according to plan.

The plan that Dan had come up with four months ago.

CHAPTER EIGHTEEN

SHE WAS GOING out of her way and she knew it, Alex thought hours later.

Her room wasn't located on this side of the inn. It was actually in the exact opposite direction and if she was truly calling it a day as she'd told her father she was when she closed down the reception area for the night, she would *not* have taken this very roundabout path. A path that took her by the dining room and the parlor, as well as allowed her to glance outside along the longest expanse of the veranda.

Although the kitchen was no longer serving meals, the dining room was still open for guests who wanted a place to simply sit and talk, who preferred doing it in a homier setting than the formal parlor.

But there was no one in either place. The guests registered at the inn were either in their rooms for the night, or had gone out for the evening and hadn't returned yet. In any case, all three areas, the dining room, the parlor and the reception alcove, not to mention the veranda, were devoid of people.

That, in this particular case, really piqued her curiosity. Where was Wyatt? Their paths hadn't really crossed for a couple of days now, other than her seeing him at a distance.

And on those occasions, he was with Ms. Carlyle, who at this point had to be setting some sort of a world record when it came to meandering down memory lane. It had been two weeks now since he began interviewing her!

However, tonight she'd seen the older woman retire early. Which Alex took to mean that Wyatt would be looking for his next culprit to interview for his book.

But he hadn't come looking for her.

That's a good thing, right? Alex asked herself.

But if it was such a good thing, why did she feel so antsy? Why was there this restlessness inside her, as if there was something just holding its breath, *waiting* for Wyatt to make some sort of a move?

In a way, it was like waiting for the other shoe to fall, only to discover that for some reason the other shoe had been attached to her foot with superglue and wasn't going to fall for a very long time. Most likely when she least expected it.

So here she was, checking around the main house, looking for a man she kept telling herself she didn't want to see.

And that was when Alex abruptly stopped, realizing that in her preoccupied state, her journey had brought her right up to Wyatt's door.

Turn around and go back! she ordered herself. If she lingered here even for a second and Wyatt should happen to open the door, she was never going to be able to live it down. She knew him. He'd razz her to the end about her stalking him—or something equally as insulting.

Alex turned on her heel when she heard it.

Heard laughter. Female laughter.

A scowl slipped over her delicate features. The laughter she heard was coming from Wyatt's room.

He wasn't supposed to have a woman in his room.

Granted, it wasn't anything that was written down, but it was definitely understood. If you checked in as a single occupancy, you remained a single occupancy.

She stood at the door, wavering for a moment and telling herself to just move on. This was none of her business and had she not gone in the most roundabout route to her own room, she wouldn't have even been aware of this.

Leaning in more closely to the door, she heard it again. That was definitely a woman laughing. Most likely some woman fawning all over Wyatt.

That in turn reminded her of the kind of wild social life he was reported to lead, according to some of the online blogs and newspapers that she'd read.

Alex blew out a breath. For a while there, with everything that had been going on, for the sorrow he'd obviously been going through, she'd temporarily forgotten about that. Forgotten about the fact that Wyatt was purportedly a playboy who changed women as often as some men changed socks.

She continued to stand, staring at the door. Wyatt deserved to be confronted. And embarrassed, she told herself, making up her mind then and there.

She knocked on his door.

Hard.

The door didn't open immediately. Was he stuffing his lady friend into a closet? Or maybe out the window? After all, he *was* on the ground floor. It wasn't all that difficult getting rid of evidence.

She was about to knock again, even more forcefully this time, when the door suddenly swung open. Without a surface for her knuckles to make contact with, she was thrown off balance.

Just like that, Alex found herself pitching forward.

And then not.

Wyatt had reacted quickly, grabbing her by her shoulders and holding her steady.

Holding her close.

He looked as surprised to see her as she was surprised by her sudden loss of balance.

"Hi. Anything I can do for you?" he asked, then added, "Other than keeping you from falling on your face, that is?"

The way he said it made her feel that he'd attached more meaning to the phrase he'd just used than she was happy about.

"Thanks," she murmured, the word all but burning a hole in her tongue.

She hated being in his debt even over something so minor. In her mind, owing him took away the balance of power and it made her feel as if she was subservient to him.

"You can let go of me now," she prompted when Wyatt didn't immediately withdraw his hands from her shoulders.

"You're sure now?" he asked, removing his hands, but holding them up so that he could grab her again in an instant. "You might just start to tip over again. Something liquid you had for dinner, perhaps?" he asked innocently.

He was implying that she was tipsy. She struggled to bank a flare of temper.

"Very funny. Does your girlfriend laugh at jokes like that? Because if she does, my guess is that you have a simpleton on your hands."

"Girlfriend?" he repeated. "You're going to have to be a little more specific than that."

"Why? Do you have more than one stashed away?" she asked, surveying the immediate area. There was no one else here, but there was always the bathroom and since the renovations some years ago, this room now had a walk-in closet. Lots of room for someone to hide.

Wyatt turned around to face her after closing the door. "The only woman in this room is you and unless you've decided to volunteer for the position of my girlfriend, I have no idea what you're talking about. As usual."

Yeah, right, as if she believed that. "I heard a woman laughing, just now."

Ah, now he knew what she was so upset about. He did what he could to look somber. "Sure that wasn't just your split personality whispering in your ear?"

"It was coming out of this room," Alex insisted through clenched teeth. "And I don't have a split personality."

"The jury hasn't come in on that one yet," he told her matter-of-factly. "Since I got here, you've been alternating between being the same lovable, haughty pain in the posterior you've always been and the really nice person my father always kept telling me you were."

Alex threw up her hands in frustration. "Now I have absolutely no idea what *you're* talking about," she snapped back at him, even though she could feel her cheeks heating and betraying her. Why couldn't she find a way to control that?

"Oh, I think you do," Wyatt contradicted, his eyes holding hers.

The distance between them didn't seem nearly wide enough for her to be able to take a full breath and she suddenly very much needed to do that.

She forced herself to focus on why she was in his room. "Okay, where's she hid-ing?" Alex pushed past him. "The woman I heard laughing just a few minutes ago, where is she?"

"Alex, there is no—oh."

"Oh," she repeated. "Care to elaborate on exactly what you mean by 'oh'?" She turned around to face him, expecting to see a very guilty look crossing his handsome features. Instead, Wyatt barely managed to suppress his laughter.

"What?" she demanded.

"I think what you heard was this." Wyatt crossed the room to a small desk.

There was a tiny recording device on the desk. He picked it up and pressed Play with his thumb as he walked back to Alex.

After a beat, the recorder in Wyatt's hand began to play.

"And then, my heart almost stopped when Clark Gable looked in my direction—and *smiled*. His wife, Carole Lombard, was definitely *not* smiling. She took him by the arm, said, 'Take me to our room, Dutchman, you've got a lot to make up for.' That was her nickname for him, you know. Not very flattering, but she was annoyed that he was paying attention to me. You have to remember, I was only a very young woman then, and much prettier than I am now."

"You're still a lovely woman," Alex heard Wyatt say. And then the sound of warm laughter filled the air.

Alex looked at Wyatt, wide-eyed. "That's Ms. Carlyle and you," she said, recognizing the two voices instantly. The laughter she'd heard belonged to Ms. Carlyle. How had she missed that?

"I was transcribing the session into the computer," he explained just in case she was going to ask why he was sitting alone in his room, listening to Anne Carlyle.

Alex wasn't thinking about the recording. She was focused on her reaction to what she'd *thought* she'd heard. A woman in Wyatt's room. And she'd been jealous, Alex reluctantly realized.

It was difficult for her to admit, even to herself, to the unexpected emotion jealousy. After a beat she confessed, "I feel like an idiot."

Wyatt shrugged, dismissing the incident

as trivial. In the old days, having her mistake his recording for a flesh-and-blood woman being in his room, well, it would have been something to crow about and hold over her head.

That is, until she'd get even with him.

But he wasn't twelve anymore. "Easy mistake to make," he told her. "Playback on this recorder is extremely clear. Through the door, it probably sounded exactly like a woman laughing in my room."

Since Wyatt was being so nice about it, it made her feel even worse. She'd had no right to jump to conclusions the way she had. "Sorry I barged in like the bed-and-breakfast police," she mumbled.

He laughed softly. "You didn't 'barge' in. I opened the door and if anything, you fell in."

That wasn't exactly an image she welcomed, but she let it pass. "Still, I must have come on like a prude to you."

His eyes held hers for a moment. "Actually, the thought never crossed my mind."

She knew for a fact that the temperature couldn't have gone up by ten degrees just now, which meant it had to be her. It was time to retreat. "I'll leave you to your work."

She didn't even get to take two steps. Wyatt caught her by the arm, holding her in place. "Listen, since you are here, why don't we discuss your schedule?"

"My schedule?" she queried.

"Well, for one thing, so that I don't wind up interfering with your day job. Or did you have a change of heart about letting me interview you?"

"You're finished with Ms. Carlyle? After only two weeks?"

Wyatt almost said that she made it sound as if the other woman was a tissue that had served its purpose and he no longer had any use for, but he refrained, knowing Alex well enough to realize that would set off a round of sharp-tongued banter. And while entertaining, right now it might ruin the delicate balance he was interested in achieving with her.

"For now I think she's told me all the stories she can remember. In some cases," he added with a smile, "she told them twice. If anything she's forgotten comes to her, I'll certainly take the time to listen, but I don't want Ms. Carlyle to feel that I'm squeezing her dry.

"In the meanwhile, I'd like to ask you and your sisters what it was like growing up with an ever-changing array of guests coming and going." Even Dorothy and Carlos, the assistant cook, had been little more than transients with the price of one night's lodging in their pockets—or less, in Dorothy's case. Both were hired on when there was little work to be had because outright charity would have been insulting. Richard Roman was a man who knew how important a sense of pride was to maintaining a person's dignity. "Did you like it? Or did you feel as if you were being invaded?"

He wasn't telling her about the sort of questions he had on his agenda, he was actually *asking* her, she realized.

"I liked it," she responded without hesitation.

"Really?" He seemed genuinely surprised. "Because I always had the impression you felt as if you were being invaded."

Now it made sense. "That wasn't because of any of the inn's guests," she told him. "That was only because of you."

"Me?" he asked. It wasn't as if he'd deliberately picked the place she called home. His father had chosen it, not him. "If having strangers come and go was acceptable, why would you feel that I was invading your home?"

"Because you were," she answered simply. "The other guests were always friendly, like visiting relatives on their best behavior because they'd be gone soon. But you were here for the first four weeks of every summer and I knew you'd just take over if I let you. So I didn't let you." It sounded uncomplicated when she said it that way, but they both knew that what had gone on between them had been far from simple.

In other words, he thought, listening to her explanation, what she'd done came under the heading of a preemptive strike. "So that was why you were always in my face."

Alex inclined her head. A coin had two sides. "Because you were always in mine."

Although, looking back, she realized now that it was all a matter of perception. She felt he was in her face, he felt she was in his. In reality, it was a little bit of both because somehow, they wound up sharing the same space, summer after summer.

The rivalry they shared had actually served him well. He wouldn't be where he was now if not for her. If not for wanting to show her up. "I suppose I should thank you."

That was *not* what she'd expected to hear Wyatt say. Not only that, but she didn't understand what he was talking about.

"Why would you want to thank me?"

"Because if it wasn't for you, I wouldn't have learned to become so competitive. You became someone I wanted to put in her place, to beat seven ways from sundown, so to speak." His desire to compete drove him to study harder, bone up on facts, try to become smarter. And there was also something else. "You're also the reason I started working out."

Now he was just making things up. "How did I do that?" she challenged.

He wondered if she really didn't know, or was just pretending. "Do you remember the first time we all went down to the beach together?"

Alex thought for a moment, then shook her head. She drew a blank.

"Sorry. No."

He still wasn't sure if he believed her. It had been such a life-changing moment for him.

"Well, I do. Vividly. I was eleven." And so insecure, it was almost terminal. "We all had our bathing suits on under our clothes and when we got to the beach, your dad said we could go swimming before lunch. When I took off my shirt, you started laughing so hard, I thought you were going to fall down. You said I was so skinny, your dad had matches for the fireplace that had more of a body than I did."

The remark, and her laughter, had really stung and had haunted him for months on end. Until he'd decided to do something about it.

Alex still didn't really remember the incident. "That was a bratty thing to say and I apologize."

"Don't," he told her. "If you hadn't made fun of me, I wouldn't have started working out as if I were possessed. And that, in turn, helped me build myself up. So in a very real sense, I have you to thank for this." The next moment, as she watched in mesmerized disbelief, Wyatt stripped off his T-shirt in one fluid motion.

And then her jaw dropped.

Thinking back now, she realized that the last time she had seen him without his shirt on was roughly around the time of the story he was telling. If he had been eleven, that made her nine, breathing down the neck of ten. What she recalled now was that he had been pale, skinny and flatter than an ironing board.

He was none of those things now.

It took her a moment to get her bearings and more than just a couple more to carefully reengage her all-but-numb tongue.

"Well, unless you're planning on going for another swim now, I think it might be a good idea if you put your shirt back on."

Before I have no kneecaps left whatsoever.

"Sorry. You're right. I get a little carried away sometimes. But all this," he paused to flex his muscles and just for a moment, part of him looked as if it was forged out of rock, "is thanks to you. So if you think I'm here to settle any old grudges between us, you can stop worrying."

"I'm not worrying," she informed him as he put the shirt back on. "Besides, you got your revenge years ago."

He had no idea what she was referring to. "And how did I do that?"

"That time when you kissed me. It was my first kiss and for exactly thirty seconds, my whole world lit up. And then you told me you kissed me because someone dared you to."

He hadn't realized that something he'd said as a kid had hurt her as much as she'd hurt him.

Since they were being honest with each other, he saw no reason to continue keeping this from her. "There was no dare," he admitted. "I only said that because I didn't want you to know how much I *wanted* to kiss you. I figured if you knew, I'd never have heard the end of it."

She was too stunned to say anything except, "Oh." That changed everything.

"I think that maybe," Wyatt began, choosing each word slowly, "we should both turn over a new leaf and start over."

"Okay," she finally replied. Her mouth had suddenly turned incredibly dry on her, as if she'd gargled with sand.

A new leaf. Why did she feel as if she'd just been put on notice?

And why did she feel as if she wasn't up to whatever was coming her way? She'd always been more than a match before. Whether it came to dealing with Wyatt or slowly taking over the running of the inn, she had always dug deep and come up with the inner resources to do what needed to be done.

He'd wanted to kiss me.

That changed *everything*.

CHAPTER NINETEEN

IT WAS A LITTLE AFTER six-thirty the next morning and although there was a part of Alex that would have loved to sleep in, she valued solitude more.

At this hour of the morning, she knew she'd have the dining room to herself. She'd be able to eat and think in peace before the day, with all its unique details and problems, could launch itself at her.

Cris was already up and working in the kitchen, preparing to make breakfast for the guests. But her other two sisters, as well as her father, were still in their rooms, sound asleep. This small island of time was perfect to her.

Or it was supposed to have been.

She carefully made her way out the kitchen doors, balancing her plate of bacon, eggs and cheese—along with white toast, orange juice and creamy coffee—on a tray.

"Is it self-serve this early in the morning?" Wyatt asked from the table she usually claimed as her own.

For a second, Alex debated setting her tray down at another table, but that would seem petulant and she didn't really want to start out on the wrong foot with him this morning. Quite frankly, after what he'd told her last night, she wasn't altogether certain *how* to react to him. Part of her wanted to continue as usual, the other part pointed out that there no longer was an "as usual" to revert to.

So she put her tray down and slid onto a seat at the table where Wyatt had already made himself right at home.

"No," she answered. "I'm just saving Cris the trouble of having to come out and serve me. She's got enough on her hands with guests' breakfasts."

"So Cris is up, too." He made a mental note of that. At this point, every detail associated with the inn was relevant until he sorted through them and decided what to use and what to discard. "Anyone else?"

"What is this, a bed check?" she asked defensively.

Way to go, Alex. Great way to start. Snap his head off why don't you?

She pressed her lips together, forcing herself to relax. "Sorry," she murmured.

"I'm just trying to orient myself as to how the inn operates," he explained, letting her apology slide.

"You grew up here," Alex said, mystified. "Didn't you notice anything in all that time?"

"I did," he replied, "but it was different, then. A kid who has to travel halfway around the continent to spend summers with his father is already busy trying to acclimate to the change of command as well as the change of scenery and time zone. But most important, back then, your father ran the inn—"

"He still does." Alex was quick to set him straight. "I just help."

A knowing smile played on his lips, as if

she'd just protested too hard. "You're Cardinal Richelieu to his Louis the XIII."

Alex's blue eyes narrowed considerably. Had they been laser beams, Wyatt had no doubt he would have been cut in two. "History regarded Richelieu as a despicable person and Louis XIII was considered an idiot."

He freely backed away. The last thing he wanted was to get into an argument with her in the first hour of the first day of them starting over.

"Okay, sorry, bad comparison," he apologized. "But if your father is still the king, as you say, you are definitely the power behind the throne."

"I make things easy for him," she corrected with a shrug. Maybe she'd been too quick to absolve Wyatt of his sins, she thought now. "Look, if this is going to work, you're going to have to stop being so critical."

That hadn't been his intent when he'd said that she was the one who made things happen at the inn. "Did you ever think that you *perceive* it as being critical when it's not intended that way?"

"No," she said flatly.

Could she really be so certain? he wondered. "Well, at least you're honest." It was a start, he supposed. "As for my part, I'll try not to sound as if I'm being critical. I'll try to behave."

Alex pretended to roll her eyes. "One can only hope."

"And you," he pointed out, "are going to have to stop that."

Alex struggled to tamp down a wave of defensiveness. *New game rules, remember?* "Stop what?"

As if she didn't know. "Those little snide, snarky comments."

Alex raised her chin. He recognized it as her defensive move. "I *do not* make snide comments and I certainly don't make snarky ones."

"Yeah, you do," he contradicted, his tone matter-of-fact rather than annoyed. "Let's just both resolve to do better," he proposed, putting his hand out to her.

She looked at it for a long moment, then finally shook it—warily.

Wyatt grinned as, after a significant beat, he dropped her hand. "Now, that wasn't so hard, was it?"

"What's going to be hard is you toeing the line," she told him.

"We," Wyatt corrected her. "We will be toeing the line." As he said it, he wondered if she was going to argue with him about this, as well.

Alex inclined her head and uttered, "We," as if the word was a bitter-tasting, rotten piece of fruit, one step away from poisoning her. But at least she'd conceded the point, he thought. For her that was a giant leap forward.

With that settled for now, Wyatt eyed her plate. She'd hardly touched her food. "You going to eat all that bacon?"

Suppressing a sigh, she turned her plate approximately ninety degrees so that the side with the bacon slices faced him.

"Help yourself."

Wyatt plucked one crispy strip from the stash, but before making it disappear into his mouth, he raised his eyes to hers and asked, "You don't mind?"

"Would it matter?" she countered.

The old Wyatt would have retorted, "No." But he'd shed that skin a long time ago. Except, old habits died hard—but they did die, he reminded himself.

"Yes, it would matter. I don't want to alienate you our first day working together."

"Too late," she said dryly, then, realized that she had been flippant when she was supposed to be trying *not* to be. "Sorry," she murmured. "This arrangement is going to take some getting used to for me."

"Ditto," he agreed. "And for the record, I meant no disrespect earlier—"

"Which earlier?" she asked in all sincerity. He'd already said a few things that she could have taken the wrong way.

"When I said you were Cardinal Richelieu. What I meant by that was that I saw you as a very capable person, someone who could take over at a moment's notice and keep things running smoothly."

Boy, talk about a spin doctor. She had to

hand it to him. "The Cardinal," she pointed out, "did it because he was power mad."

"Some say he did it because he wanted France to stay strong, be respected, do well. See the similarity?" he asked.

"Put that way…okay," she admitted, "you weren't trying to be insulting." She nodded at the bacon that was still on her plate. "You can have more if you want. Or just ask Cris to make up a plate for you. You can have whatever you want, you know."

Too late, Alex realized that she'd just given him far too much of a straight line to resist, even if he was on his best behavior.

"I already have it," he answered. "I like nibbling off your plate."

She moved the plate so that it was between the two of them. It struck her that there was something rather intimate about sharing breakfast this way—even if it was with Wyatt.

Who are you kidding with that little coda? It feels intimate because it is with Wyatt, an annoying little voice in her head said before she could successfully block it out.

"So, how are we going to do this?" she asked. "Are you going to ask me a set of questions, or do I just start talking?"

The last part of the question made him grin. "You mean, you haven't already?"

"What's that supposed to mean?" The defensive edge was back in her voice.

"That was a joke. But to answer your question, what I mean to do is just follow you around, shadow your day exactly as it happens."

That wasn't what she thought she had signed on for. "I thought you wanted to hear stories about the inn."

Maybe he needed to explain his concept of the project a little more fully. "This is a story about the inn, as it's unfolding. Ms. Carlyle gave me a lot of good background, as did your dad—"

Alex looked at him in obvious surprise. "When did you interview my dad?"

"I didn't," he said. "My father did. It's all there in his notes—and in the diary."

"What diary? This is the first mention of a diary that I've heard of."

Wyatt had a feeling that no one had known about the diary—except, perhaps, for Alex's father. "The diary my father kept about his summers here. He started it as a journal right after he and my mother were divorced. He first showed it to me just before he died."

It was really difficult for him to talk about this, but he needed to be able to get past the sharp peaks of pain if he was going to keep the promise he'd made to his father. "He said he started it as a way to try to figure out just what went wrong, but it wound up being a diary of the all times he spent here with me. He told me that, after he…passed on, I should read it."

She knew that if it was her and her father had given her a diary like that, she would have had trouble reading the entries so soon after his death.

Wyatt was stronger than she'd thought.

"And did you?" she asked.

He nodded, absently breaking off another piece of bacon and popping it in his mouth. "Took me a couple of weeks to work up my nerve, but yes, I finally read it a few days ago."

"And?" she prompted.

"And, aside from a great many anecdotes about the inn, I discovered that my father and I shared a lot of the same values. He was only about eight years older than I was when he started keeping this diary or journal, whatever you want to call it. A lot of what he went through I can see myself reacting to the same way."

He smiled, more to himself than her, remembering a passage he'd read that struck home. "It makes me feel closer to him." And then he looked at her, realizing the tactical error he'd just committed. He'd handed her something that she could use against him. "But you probably think that's hokey."

Just exactly what did he think of her? Did he see her as some kind of malicious harpy? "No, why would I?"

"Because you kind of...barrel through life, you know? Like a...like a...steamroller, and steamrollers aren't exactly known for their sensitivity. Or rather their tolerance of sensitivity."

This was just getting better and better, she thought. "You see me as an insensitive steamroller?"

Maybe he shouldn't have said that—but it was too late to take the words back now. "Honestly?"

Alex drew herself up where she sat. "That's what I assume we're supposed to be being."

Okay, he had no one to blame for this but himself. "Then yes, I do. But lately…"

His voice trailed off, but he had really piqued her curiosity.

"Lately?" Alex prompted, waiting for him to finish his thought and bracing herself just in case she didn't like what he would say. And it hadn't gotten off to a promising start, to put it mildly.

"Lately I've been seeing glimmers of a much softer woman beneath the bravado. One who, although she talks about being independent and being her own person, I think also wants to share her life with someone else."

She didn't like how close to the truth he'd gotten. That was a side of her she'd thought she'd kept successfully under wraps. A side that had reacted very badly to being made fun of by a little boy she'd had a crush on.

Any bridges that he had begun constructing between them were in danger of crumbling now. "You never told me you took psych courses in college."

His eyes held hers and she felt as if he was looking into her very soul. And seeing secrets he shouldn't.

"Just something I picked up along the way."

"Along the way?" Was there some sort of double meaning to that?

"Through life," he replied. "Lessons all leave a deeper impression when they're learned that way." He looked down at Alex's plate and realized he had all but picked it clean. "Sorry," he apologized. "I didn't realize I'd eaten that much. Let me go and see if I can rustle up some more for you."

But as he started to get up, she stopped him. "No, don't bother Cris. It's okay."

"I wasn't planning on bothering Cris."

But he just said he was going to bring her back another serving of breakfast. "Then what were you planning on doing?"

The expression on his face said he would have thought she'd put two and two together by now. "Making it for you, if Cris doesn't have any objections to another pair of hands in the kitchen."

Alex stared at him. "You're telling me you can cook?"

"Not enough for Julia Child to claim me as her long-lost grandson, but well enough to keep myself alive if need be." As he left the table, Wyatt glanced at her over his shoulder and laughed. "Close your mouth, Alex. That's not your most attractive look."

Embarrassed, Alex quickly closed her mouth and rose from the table. "This I've got to see," she announced, following him.

He took her skepticism in stride. "Sure. You can even pitch in if you want."

He probably thought he could get her to do it for him. She would have—if he hadn't said that he was capable of doing it himself.

"Oh, no, you're on your own here," she

told him. "I just want to observe, and make sure you don't burn down the kitchen."

It had been a long time since he had failed at something he set out to do and if she was waiting for that, she was going to be disappointed.

"Haven't done it yet," he replied, "so I wouldn't hold my breath if I were you."

"I'm not holding my breath," she protested with just a touch of indignation.

But he knew better. "Yes, you are. I think you really enjoy the thought of my falling on my face."

"Not falling—tripping a little, maybe," she conceded, "but not a complete pratfall."

"You know, this new-leaf thing of yours is refreshing." Although, he had to admit it took some getting used to after all those years of always being wary that she was setting him up for something.

"Just remember you said that. You might not find it so refreshing after I tell you what I think of your cooking efforts," she warned.

Her comment didn't faze him. Wyatt

held the kitchen door open for her. "Prepare to be amazed."

"What I'm preparing for is to be amused."

He laughed.

That odd, rippling sensation started up in her stomach.

She was definitely going to have to watch her step, Alex cautioned herself, even as she followed him into the kitchen.

CHAPTER TWENTY

CRIS WAS AT her worktable when they opened the door into her domain.

"Back again?" she asked before she realized that this time Alex wasn't alone.

"Interview over already?" Cris ventured as she shook her head. "This has to be some kind of record, even for you two."

"The interview hasn't even begun yet," Wyatt informed her.

"Oh, then what can I do for you, Wyatt?" Cris asked, indicating the stove.

Wyatt waved her back to her work.

"Nothing," he told her. "Just continue doing whatever you were doing. I'm going to make your sister a replacement breakfast. I got carried away out there and I seem to have eaten all of hers."

"Oh." This time, Alex read the amusement in her sister's expression. "Well, then, I can—"

"No," Wyatt interrupted before she could complete the offer. "*I* can. You've got more than enough to do, Cris. The inn is booked solid—again—and my guess, since you have the gift of making even shoe leather taste out of this world, is that they'll all be coming down for their complimentary breakfast sometime between seven and ten, so you'd better get ready. Don't worry," he assured her, "I know my way around bacon, scrambled eggs and toast well enough not to get lost."

Alex saw Cris glance in her direction with this wide, know-it-all grin. She followed that up by looking at Wyatt next and giving him her blessings with a gesture that indicated he had the run of her kitchen for as long as he needed it.

"Okay, Wyatt, have at it," she said.

Alex had the distinct feeling that her sister wasn't just referring to the kitchen when she said "it," but that somehow she was being included in that grouping.

Wasn't *anyone* on her side?

FOR THE NEXT five weeks—for Alex—it felt as if every day began and ended with Wyatt.

He was there, shadowing her, sometimes to ask questions, sometimes just to observe her going through the paces of her day. Within a few days it quickly got to the point that if Wyatt wasn't with her, she'd catch herself looking around, waiting for him to pop up.

He really did drive her crazy at times, but just when his questions delved too deep and she was on the verge of telling him that she wasn't going to put up with his burrowing into her life anymore, he'd back off. It was as if he could actually sense what she was thinking.

She wasn't the only one Wyatt talked to. All three of her sisters were observed, as was her father. But from what Alex could tell, the time Wyatt spent questioning her family seemed to be minimal while the time he spent questioning her seemed to go on and on.

And on.

While she tried to act as if she resented the

constant and never-ending intrusion on her time, Alex had to admit in the privacy of her own mind that she had grown accustomed to it in a remarkably short amount of time.

The most incredible thing about her reversal of attitude toward him was that when she remembered an incident—or she'd seen a photograph in his father's private album that subsequently triggered a memory— she actually went looking for Wyatt so she could tell him about it.

And somewhere around the fourth week it occurred to her, although she tried to bury the thought, that she was going to miss Wyatt. She'd miss talking to him when he finally accumulated what he needed to do justice to the inn's history—and left.

Because Labor Day was almost here, Alex had a feeling that the day of Wyatt's departure wasn't that far away.

She tried to brace herself for it, but even as she did, she wondered if perhaps this was a losing proposition.

"YOU KNOW," ALEX said one evening after dinner as she and Wyatt sat on the veranda in the oversize white wicker chairs. "I didn't even know your dad had an album like that. All those photographs he'd taken of us and the inn."

She remembered Uncle Dan snapping a camera every so often, but she had never once seen any of the photographs he'd taken.

The evening air was almost silky, and Wyatt took his time answering her. "He didn't."

That didn't make any sense. "But you showed me the album," she protested. If it hadn't belonged to his father, then whose was it?

"What my dad had was a large box full of pictures."

"Now that I think of it, that sounds more like him," she said with a fond laugh. "But if he hadn't put those photos into the album you showed me, then who—?"

"I did. When I found that box of pictures, I decided to surprise my father with the album."

He had stayed up all night doing it,

knowing he was racing the clock because his father had told him he was dying.

"The one good thing he did—other than take the photographs—was write the date on the back of each and every one of them, so I was able to put it in chronological order.

"I finished it two days before he…" Wyatt cleared his throat and attempted to finish his sentence again, but he failed a second time.

Moved by the emotion Wyatt was trying to ignore, Alex covered his hand with her own. "I know," she said quietly. There was no need to say anything further, no reason to call death by its name. "That was a really nice thing for you to do for him." She paused for a moment, then added, "So is finishing this book."

Wyatt could relive the scene when his father had asked him to do it at the drop of a hat. "He was really adamant about that. Held on to my hand until I promised him that I would finish the book. He smiled at me after I said it and really looked at peace for the first time since he'd told me about his diagnosis. As gruesome as it sounds, it was as if I'd just given him permission to die."

Alex thought about that for a moment. "Maybe, in a way, you did. Uncle Dan always finished his assignments, lived up to his commitments, brought in an article before deadline. He took pride in those things. Knowing the book he was contracted to write would be sent to his publisher after his death meant that he was keeping his side of the bargain."

Wyatt laughed shortly. The expression on his face made him appear to be a million miles away. And maybe he was, Alex thought. "You're probably right. Funny thing was, when I called his publisher to see if he still wanted the book, the guy told me my father had already spoken to him and pitched me as a replacement author weeks prior to my call. He was completely on board."

Wyatt paused, taking a deep breath, as if to clear his head.

What he was really looking to do was change the subject. "You know, you never told me why you came back to the inn after college."

"What do you mean, why did I come back? Because this is my home."

That wasn't really enough. "You were twenty-two with degrees in business administration and accounting. You could have gone anywhere with them. Your friend Stacy did," Wyatt pointed out.

"My dad was still having health problems at the time, but he wouldn't take it easy," she confided. "I couldn't just go off, looking to have some big adventure, not when he needed me. Besides," she added with a shrug, "I'd be spending all my time worrying about him and flunk all my interviews. Nobody would hire someone who was preoccupied to help run their business."

"Rothchild and Saunders wanted to hire you, as did Eleventh Hour," Wyatt said, mentioning the names of two high-end, exclusive companies.

The pleasant evening talk they had been having immediately took a nosedive.

"You *investigated* me?" she cried,

stunned. Why would he do that? Whatever the answer to that was, she knew she didn't appreciate her past being dug up and examined.

"No, your father mentioned it to me during one of our talks. He felt guilty about you giving up those opportunities and, at the same time, he was proud of you for being so selfless and making that kind of sacrifice for the inn."

"I didn't do it for the inn," she told him quite truthfully—she didn't want any praise under false pretenses. "I did it for my dad. And I'd do it again," she added with feeling. "In a heartbeat. Except that now I'd probably do it for the inn, as well. The inn is in my blood," she admitted freely. "I realize now that it's part of who I am."

Wyatt nodded. "I think you're right."

That surprised her. And yet, she had to admit that these past few weeks she'd spent with Wyatt had been one surprise after another. Five weeks had gone by and they were both still standing—and unscathed. Not just that, but even more astonishing, she *liked* spending time with him.

Alex paused now for a moment, waging an internal war with herself. She was struggling not to broach the subject that was foremost in her mind; best to let sleeping dogs lie. But she needed to have every question answered, every magic trick explained. Her curiosity had to be appeased, and she wanted to ask him just how much longer he would be here, researching and writing.

The side that needed to know won.

And lost.

Because when she asked, Wyatt told her what she *didn't* want to hear. "Actually, I've got everything I came for, so I'll be leaving, ironically, on Labor Day."

She felt her stomach seize up. She did her best to ignore it and the restlessness and distress that washed over her, threatening to completely unravel her composure.

Words were sticking to the roof of her mouth as she said, "I thought…you were supposed to write the book…while you were staying here."

"I did. All except for the end of the last chapter," he added. "And it's still a rough draft, but it came together pretty well. It won't take much to polish it up, dot the i's, cross the t's, that sort of thing. The publisher wants it by the end of the week."

"The end of the week," she echoed, the phrase all but throbbing in her brain. Wyatt was leaving at the end of the week. He wouldn't be around to haunt her every move, wouldn't be there to pop up in the most awkward places, making her feel as if every single space of her life had been invaded.

She was, in effect, getting her life back.

So why didn't that make her happy?

THE NEXT COUPLE of days seemed almost surreal. The minutes seemed to evaporate even before they arrived, taking the hours hostage, making them, too, disappear before they could adequately register.

Alex felt like someone who was trying to hold on to raindrops with her bare hands. It just wasn't working. The raindrops were seeping through her fingers.

She hardly saw Wyatt.

He spent most of his last two days at the

inn with her father. Something about needing to clarify a few more points.

She already missed him, which wasn't
possible because he was still here. A person
had to be out of sight to be missed, right?

She didn't know.

Alex wasn't certain about anything anymore. Moreover, the confidence she'd had
in herself, in the way she ran the inn, in
the way she faced each day, now felt as if
it was actually perched on a foundation of
wet sand instead of concrete.

It's a trick, it's all smoke and mirrors.
Wyatt got to you somehow, but once he's
gone, you'll be able to detoxify and every-
thing will be fine again, you'll see.

She should be counting the seconds until
Wyatt was gone, not trying to harvest the
minutes he was still here.

The pep talk did no good.

Alex found herself at loose ends and
those ends were swiftly coming unrav-
eled. Somehow, rather than attending to
the inn's books the way she was supposed
to be doing, Alex suddenly discovered herself drifting by Wyatt's room—she refused

to admit that she'd gotten there by design—
and then knocking on his door before she
could stop herself.

"C'mon in," Wyatt called out. "It's open."

Even so, there was a quick tug-of-war
in her brain, urging her to run before she
eased the door open, pushing it with her
fingertips.

Wyatt was by the bed, throwing a couple
of things into the suitcase that lay sprawled
open on the quilted comforter.

"You're packing."

Wyatt laughed. "There's that keen eye
of yours again."

Alex heard herself saying, "So I guess
that this is really goodbye."

Wyatt folded his extra pair of jeans and
deposited them into the suitcase. "I prefer my father's way of saying it. 'See you
soon,'" he added.

As if she needed to be reminded. As if
she'd ever forget what words his father said
at the end of each summer vacation, before
the pair left the inn and Wyatt would be put
back on a plane to New York.

"Yes, but when he said that," Alex

pointed out, even as she struggled against the wave of sadness she felt swelling within her, "it was understood that there *would* be a later."

Wyatt stopped packing for a moment to look at her. "What makes you think that there isn't?"

Why was he making her spell it out? They both knew he wouldn't be coming back. That this very well could be the last time they would see each other. Maybe he didn't care, but she did—and she hated him for it.

"Because your dad's not around anymore so there's no reason for you to come back and spend the summer here, and the book is done."

"The book might be," Wyatt readily admitted, "but I'm not. I've still got some unfinished business to tend to."

Was he setting her up for a punch line, or was he telling her that he really intended to come back to the inn? Alex was afraid to allow herself to entertain the idea, afraid to hope because the letdown would be too fierce.

She needed to leave the room.

She couldn't.

"Like what?" she asked, her breath stuck in her throat.

Wyatt looked at her for a long moment, wondering if he was making a fatal mistake. His brain told him he might be, but his gut was weighing in with another answer. When it came to choosing a side between his brain and his gut, he'd always gone with his gut.

Now was no exception.

"Like trying to find out why my pulse races the way it does whenever you're around—and it's not because I want to strangle you the way I used to," he added with just the smallest of smiles.

"No strangling," she said. Was he telling her that he'd felt the dynamics between them changing the way she had? The corners of her mouth insisted on curving up. She seemed to have no control over that lately, she noticed. Or, it seemed, over the way she felt about Wyatt. "Does this mean I'm safe with you?"

For the time being, he abandoned the

idea of packing and crossed over to her. He slipped his arms around her. "Oh, I wouldn't exactly say that. People say I'm a dangerous guy."

It wasn't his arms that held her in place. It was what she saw in his eyes. She saw her destiny—and it didn't frighten her the way she'd once secretly suspected that it might. "Do they, now?"

"Absolutely." Wyatt did his best to keep a straight face.

"You know," she told him as she tilted her head up just a tad, "I've always found 'dangerous' to be kind of exciting."

He gave up trying not to smile. It was just too hard when every fiber of his being was already grinning inside him. "Then we're good," he said as he lowered his lips to hers.

"Very good," she murmured just before their lips made contact.

But it wasn't very good, she discovered. It was excellent.

EPILOGUE

RICHARD ROMAN SLOWLY made his way down the slight slope and went directly to the family cemetery.

In the past, when he came here, it was to talk to his wife, to give Amy an update on the girls, or to share a special moment with her, the way he had when she was alive and by his side.

The headstone had a carving of an angel on it. An angel that had her face. Talking to the headstone made him feel somehow closer to Amy.

But today he didn't stop at her grave, beyond saying a quick hello and asking her indulgence because today, he had come to talk to Dan.

The corners of Richard's mouth curved into a sad smile as he looked down on the newest headstone in the relatively small plot of land. At Dan's request, the headstone was basic and straightforward, very much like the man himself had been.

"Well, as usual, you were right, old friend," Richard said, addressing the headstone. "Your plan worked just the way you hoped it would."

He remembered thinking that he'd had his doubts, despite Dan's optimism. But Dan was certain. He'd felt that his deathbed request would force his son to be with Alex on a constant basis and dissolve whatever false barriers were in the way. Given their daily close contact, the sharp edges of their banter would wear away and they would finally have to admit that they had feelings for each other. Feelings that ran deep.

"They're getting married next month. Wyatt popped the question last night when he came to tell us that your book would be coming out next April, just in time to celebrate the inn's 120th anniversary." His smile widened. "He asked, and Alex had the good sense to say yes. Our kids are getting married," he said with mingled pride and excitement.

Richard laughed softly. "You certainly called it. I always wanted them together, but I never thought it was going to happen. But you, you knew exactly how to do it. And now, looking back, it all seems so simple.

"Too bad you can't be here for the ceremony, but I guess that was all part of it, wasn't it? Making Wyatt feel obligated to work on the book you started because you told him how much it meant to you.

"That way, no matter how much he wanted to just walk away from Alex and never look back, he couldn't. And because they were involved in doing this one last project for you, they finally saw beyond all their clever rhetoric and fell in love just the way you said they would. I don't mind saying it again—I was wrong—but you, you never doubted. You knew."

Richard sighed heavily. He missed hearing Dan's deep voice, missed talking over old times with the one person who'd shared all those old times with him.

"And I'd give everything I own just to have you down here at the wedding." His sad smile deepened. "But I guess you'll have a ringside seat for it, won't you?

"Got a favor to ask, since you're up there. Watch out for my Amy, will you? Look after my girl until I get there and can do it myself, okay?"

He assumed that if Dan could say something, the answer would have been yes.

"I miss you both," Richard said with another heavy sigh. And then he glanced toward the inn. "I've got to be getting back before Alex comes looking for me," he said to the headstone. "Stevi's declared dibs on making the wedding arrangements and someone's got to be there to rein that girl in. I'd appreciate a few hints whispered in my ear on how to do that when you get the chance. You were always so much better at getting people to listen to you than I ever was.

"That's all for now," Richard concluded. "But I'll be back to give you and Amy an update when I get the chance." He smiled at the headstone and said, "Well, see you later," as he turned and took his leave.

Like an old friend, the timeless sound of the waves rhythmically moving in to the shore and then out again accompanied him as he went back to the inn.

* * * * *

REQUEST YOUR FREE BOOKS!
2 FREE WHOLESOME ROMANCE NOVELS
IN LARGER PRINT
PLUS 2
FREE
MYSTERY GIFTS

✻✻✻✻✻✻✻✻✻✻✻✻✻✻✻✻✻✻✻✻✻✻✻✻✻

HEARTWARMING™

✻✻✻✻✻✻✻✻✻✻✻✻✻✻✻✻✻✻✻✻✻✻✻✻✻

Wholesome, tender romances

YES! Please send me 2 FREE Harlequin® Heartwarming Larger-Print novels and my 2 FREE mystery gifts (gifts worth about $10). After receiving them, if I don't wish to receive any more books, I can return the shipping statement marked "cancel." If I don't cancel, I will receive 4 brand-new larger-print novels every month and be billed just $4.99 per book in the U.S. or $5.74 per book in Canada. That's a savings of at least 23% off the cover price. It's quite a bargain! Shipping and handling is just 50¢ per book in the U.S. and 75¢ per book in Canada.* I understand that accepting the 2 free books and gifts places me under no obligation to buy anything. I can always return a shipment and cancel at any time. Even if I never buy another book, the two free books and gifts are mine to keep forever.

161/361 IDN F47N

Name	(PLEASE PRINT)
Address	Apt. #
City	State/Prov.	Zip/Postal Code

Signature (if under 18, a parent or guardian must sign)

Mail to the **Harlequin® Reader Service:**
IN U.S.A.: P.O. Box 1867, Buffalo, NY 14240-1867
IN CANADA: P.O. Box 609, Fort Erie, Ontario L2A 5X3

* Terms and prices subject to change without notice. Prices do not include applicable taxes. Sales tax applicable in N.Y. Canadian residents will be charged applicable taxes. Offer not valid in Quebec. This offer is limited to one order per household. Not valid for current subscribers to Harlequin Heartwarming larger-print books. All orders subject to credit approval. Credit or debit balances in a customer's account(s) may be offset by any other outstanding balance owed by or to the customer. Please allow 4 to 6 weeks for delivery. Offer available while quantities last.

Your Privacy—The Harlequin® Reader Service is committed to protecting your privacy. Our Privacy Policy is available online at www.ReaderService.com or upon request from the Harlequin Reader Service.

We make a portion of our mailing list available to reputable third parties that offer products we believe may interest you. If you prefer that we not exchange your name with third parties, or if you wish to clarify or modify your communication preferences, please visit us at www.ReaderService.com/consumerschoice or write to us at Harlequin Reader Service Preference Service, P.O. Box 9062, Buffalo, NY 14269. Include your complete name and address.

HWDIR13R

ReaderService.com

Manage your account online!

- Review your order history
- Manage your payments
- Update your address

> ## *We've designed the Harlequin® Reader Service website just for you.*

Enjoy all the features!

- Reader excerpts from any series
- Respond to mailings and special monthly offers
- Discover new series available to you
- Browse the Bonus Bucks catalog
- Share your feedback

Visit us at:
ReaderService.com